THE LEGEND OF NIMWAY HALL: 1794 - CHARLOTTE

KAREN HAWKINS

The Legend of Nimway Hall: 1974 - Charlotte
Copyright © 2018 by Karen Hawkins
ISBN-13: 978-1986589833
ISBN-10: 1986589838

NYLA Publishing
121 W 27th St., Suite 1201, New York, NY 10001
http://www.nyliterary.com

ABOUT THIS BOOK

1794: CHARLOTTE

*New York Times bestselling author Karen Hawkins writes a ravishing
addition to an exciting series of romances touched by magic as old
as time.*

*A properly raised young lady rebels against the restrictions of both
society and family when she meets a dark, dangerous, and wildly
passionate man as they both fight to resist their forbidden love ... and the
seductive pull of an ancient magic.*

Miss Charlotte Harrington knows what's expected of her. Properly raised and newly reminded of her duties after the unexpected death of her far-more-perfect twin sister, Charlotte is resigned to wedding the son of a near neighboring land owner and live a sedate and proper, respectable life. But Charlotte's high spirits will not be contained and she yearns deeply for a life of adventure, excitement, and love.

When wild and untamed Marco di Rossi arrives at Nimway

Hall, commissioned to carve a masterpiece for the family home, he finds himself instantly drawn to the far-from-subdued Charlotte. Despite the potential ruin to his own brilliant career, he cannot resist her spirit and beauty, nor the call of the deep, wild magic that resides within a mysterious and magical orb hidden deep in the walls of the ancient house of Nimway...

THE LEGEND OF NIMWAY HALL

A love invested with mystery and magic sends ripples through the ages.

~

Long ago in a cave obscured by the mists of time, Nimue, a powerful sorceress and Merlin's beloved, took the energy of their passion and wove it into a potent love spell. Intending the spell to honor their love and enshrine it in immortality, she merged the spell into the large moonstone in the headpiece of Merlin's staff. Thus, when Merlin was far from her, he still carried the aura of their love with him and, so they both believed, the moonstone would act as a catalyst for true love, inciting and encouraging love to blossom in the hearts of those frequently in the presence of the stone.

Sadly, neither Merlin nor Nimue, despite all their power, foresaw the heart of Lancelot. A minor adept, he sensed both the presence of the spell in the moonstone and also the spell's immense power. Driven by his own desires, Lancelot stole the headpiece and used the moonstone's power to sway Guinevere to his side.

Furious that the spell crafted from the pure love of his and his beloved's hearts had been misused, Merlin smote Lancelot and seized back the headpiece. To protect it forevermore, Merlin laid upon the stone a web of control that restricted its power. Henceforth, it could act only in response to a genuine need for true love, and only when that need impacted one of his and Nimue's blood, no matter how distant.

Ultimately, Merlin sent the headpiece back to Nimue for safe keeping. As the Lady of the Lake, at that time, she lived in a cottage on an island surrounded by swiftly flowing streams, and it was in her power to see and watch over their now-dispersed offspring.

Time passed, and even those of near-immortality faded and vanished.

The land about Nimue's cottage drained, and the region eventually became known as Somerset.

Generations came and went, but crafted of spelled gold, the headpiece endured and continued to hold and protect the timeless moonstone imbued with Nimue's and Merlin's spells...

Over time, a house, crafted of sound local stone and timbers from the surrounding Balesboro Wood, was built on the site of Nimue's cottage. The house became known as Nimway Hall. From the first, the house remained in the hands and in the care of a female descendant of Nimue, on whom devolved the responsibilities of guardian of Nimway Hall. As decades and then centuries passed, the tradition was established that in each generation, the title of and responsibility for the house and associated estate passed to the eldest living and willing daughter of the previous female holder of the property, giving rise to the line of the Guardians of Nimway Hall.

THE GUARDIANS OF NIMWAY HALL
Nimue - Merlin.
through the mists of time

Moira Elizabeth O'Shannessy b. 1692
m. 1720 Phillip Tregarth

Jacqueline Vivienne Tregarth b. 1726
m. 1750 Lord Richard Devries

Olivia Heather Devries b. 1751
m. 1771 John "Jack" Harrington

Charlotte Anne Harrington b. 1776
m. 1794 Marco de Rossi

Isabel Jacqueline de Rossi b. 1797
m. 1818 Adam Driscoll

Miranda Rose Driscoll b. 1819
m. 1839 Michael Eades

Georgia Isabel Eades b. 1841
m. 1862 Frederick Hayden

Alexandra Edith Hayden b. 1864
m. 1888 Robert Curtis, Viscount Brynmore

Fredericka "Freddy" Viviane Curtis b. 1890
m. 1912 Anthony Marshall

Maddie Rose Devries b. 1904
m. 1926 Declan Maclean

Jocelyn Regina Stirling b. 1918
m.1940 Lt. Col. Gideon Fletcher

CHAPTER 1

"Lady Barton, are we there yet?"

Reclining on the coach seat, Verity kept her eyes closed. She was trying her best to nap and the last thing she wanted was to be drawn into conversation.

Sadly, her maid, the tall and angular Lucy Mull, had other ideas. She repeated herself in a louder voice and added, "I vow, but we've been in this coffin of a coach for nigh on ten hours now! We must be close."

That was too much, even for Verity, who prized her naps almost as much as she did her morning cup of hot chocolate. She opened her eyes and favored her maid with an angry glare. "Is the coach still moving?"

Lucy sniffed. "It is, my lady, as you well know."

"Then we are not yet at Nimway Hall! Now hush, you pestilent maid, and let me sleep!" Lady Verity tugged her feathered hat further down so that it shaded her eyes and then snuggled deeper into the puffy squabs.

Lucy gave an irritated sniff. "If you ask me, we will *never* get there what with the rain that poured down early this morning, and on roads so poor it's a disgrace to even call them such, while this box sways and swerves as if it's missing a wheel, and—"

"For the love of—" Verity shoved her hat from her eyes and sat upright. "Stop this caterwauling at once! I cannot sleep for the noise."

Lucy folded her thin lips. "I was not caterwauling. I was just saying—"

"Lud, don't repeat it! We will arrive when we will arrive. And you have not been in this 'box,' as you call my lovely coach, for ten hours. We didn't leave the inn until well after eleven this morning and it's barely three now, plus we stopped for over an hour for lunch."

Lucy said in a grumpy tone, "It *feels* as if we've been in here for ten hours." The whip-thin maid with her tight brown curls and permanent scowl was as cantankerous as a recovering drunk, but she was also as loyal as the day was long, and possessed an uncanny genius for repairing gowns and designing coifs. For those reasons, and because Verity shuddered to think of the effort she'd have to expend to train a new maid, Lucy's complaining was tolerated. Verity loved many things but expending herself was not one of them.

She wilted back into her corner of the coach and delicately covered her yawn with her plump hand. "I wish you hadn't awoken me. I was having a lovely dream involving lemon cake and Lord Rackingham."

Lucy's irritation vanished and she leaned forward eagerly. "Was it a *naughty* dream, my lady? Lord Rackingham is as handsome as they come."

"Lud, no!" Verity patted her mussed curls. "Not this time, anyway." *More's the pity.*

Lucy looked as disappointed as Verity felt. The maid said in a wistful tone, "I had a dream about Lord Rackingham once. He was naked, he was, and bold as a pirate, too."

"I'm sure he was, for he seems to have tendencies in that direction. But please, do not say another word. I have to meet that man in public and I've no wish to think of—"

"There I was, in a stone tower, locked behind a huge door, and reclining on a divan like a princess in a cream silk gown that was open from my chin to my ankles. Wide open it was, too."

"I daresay you were chilly."

"I think I was, now that you mention it," Lucy admitted. "And then Lord Rackingham arrived. He *kicked* down the door and, sword drawn, *burst* into my room naked as the day he was born—"

"Wait. He was already naked? Before he even entered the room?"

"He was."

"And yet he *broke* down a heavy door? With his bare hands?"

"Aye, so he did."

"Was he bleeding, then? I can't imagine he could break down a door whilst naked and not bruise or at least scratch himself. And why was his sword drawn? Did he expect to fight you? I vow, Lucy, but that dream makes no sense. At least my dreams make sense."

Lucy sputtered. "You dreamt last week that you owned a tiny elephant that fit in your teacup!"

"A *tiny* elephant. Which is why it fit. I didn't, however, dream about a naked man knocking down a heavy wooden door without marring his skin, and running in with a drawn sword for no reason at all. I mean, how did he knock down the door if he wasn't even wearing stiff boots in order to kick—" The coach slowed, and then turned. Verity brightened. "Ah, we must be on the drive to Nimway Hall." She pushed back the curtain to expose a beautiful forest. "Balesboro Wood, so we're close. We shall be having tea soon, which is good, for I'm famished."

The maid peered out the window, her eyebrows lowered. "There's a darkness in these woods."

"Of course there is. Woods are notoriously unfriendly places to be. They're damp, and dirty, and contain all sorts of creatures, some of whom bite. Fortunately, we shall only see it when we come and go, and then from the safety of a coach." Verity dropped the curtains back in place. "The house itself is quite lovely, and I hear my sister-in-law Olivia, who is the guardian of Nimway, has been redecorating it, so it's vastly improved from the last time I was here."

The maid frowned. "Mrs. Harrington is the guardian and not your brother?"

"Yes. The whole thing's quite complicated, and I won't pretend I understand, but Nimway Hall is always held by a female. Something to do with the entail or – Lud, I've no idea. Anyway, it's Olivia's, and one day, I suppose it will belong to Charlotte now that her sister Caroline is—" Verity closed her lips over the rest of her sentence, unable to give voice to the fact even eleven long months after the fact.

"Now that Miss Caroline is no longer with the living," Lucy offered helpfully.

Tears burned Verity's eyes, and she nodded.

"That's an odd thing, to leave the house to the female line rather than the male."

Grateful for a distraction, Verity agreed. "Indeed. From what Olivia has said, Nimway's line of succession was determined in ancient times. In fact – and do not ask me if this is true, for I've no idea – but some of the villagers say the house and lands have something to do with Merlin."

"The sorcerer?" Lucy gawped. "You cannot mean it!"

"Oh yes. Local lore says that the love of his life was a witch named Nimway, so the house must have been hers, although I don't think it's that old, so perhaps she owned the land or—or— Well, I've no idea. It's all rumor, of course, but a fun one."

"You don't know it's a rumor." Lucy cocked her eye at her employer. "You said yesterday that you'd visited the Hall many times. Have *you* seen any magic whilst staying here?"

"Lud, no. I never saw anything untoward. Well, except—"

Verity wondered if she should mention that day, for it had been long, long ago and, to be honest, over time she'd come to wonder if her memory hadn't been compromised by wine or—or—well, she wouldn't say 'age' as that would be too much and she was only 30(ish).

Lucy's eyes widened. "*What* did you see?"

"Nothing. At one time, I thought—" A strand of light broke through the crack in the curtain, so Verity slid it all of the way open. "There is Nimway Hall now!"

Lucy peered at the house sitting on a rise before them. "It's nowhere near as large as Chatsworth."

"Few houses are," Verity returned sharply. "Nimway Hall is not as large, but it's still quite pretty." Her family pride roused, she added, "In fact, I would say it's *prettier* than Chatsworth."

Lucy wrinkled her nose, and then muttered something under her breath that sounded like "I can't imagine that!" but must have been something far less impudent.

"You obviously aren't trying," Verity said. Her beloved brother and his dear wife had found their happiness within the walls of Nimway. Besides, who wouldn't adore such an old, stately house? The real problem was that Lucy had no appreciation for architectural majesty.

Verity looked up at the house and admired its position upon a wide bluff, a silvered pool of mist swirling at its feet. Nimway Hall was built of local stone that shimmered under the wan sun. It was three stories high with an expanse of jewel green lawn that rolled gently down to the wood that encircled it. But as beautiful as the front lawn was, Verity knew the back lawn was even more beckoning with its green grass and beautifully cultivated gardens, all framing sparkling Lake Myrrdin. Ah, how she looked forward to seeing it all from the comfort of a settee near a large, open window.

The coach continued to the house, the scent rising from the lavender bushes that lined the drive and lifting Verity's spirits. As they approached the forecourt, the mist curled away as if making a path for them. It was enough to give one the shivers, if one believed in such nonsense, which Verity most certainly didn't. Besides, her real concern wasn't with the house or the silly rumors one heard about it, but with the person waiting on them. *Oh Charlotte, my favorite and now only niece, I wonder how these past months have changed you?*

"My lady, you look sad. Missing Miss Caroline, are you?"

"It is odd, being here without her. But as difficult as it is for me and the rest of the family, I'm convinced it has been a hundred times harder for her sister Charlotte. They were twins and no two sisters were closer."

"I didn't know they were twins. It's tragic, when someone dies so young, but that makes it even worse." Lucy hesitated, and then said, "If you don't mind me asking, how did Miss Caroline die?"

"She was out riding in the woods late at night. Something must have startled her horse, for she fell and hit her head upon a rock."

"Riding after dark?" Lucy shook her head. "Young people can be so foolish."

"'Foolish' is not a word I ever thought to use to describe Caroline. The child never broke a rule, said a cross word, or did anything other than what was expected. My brother always said she was born a lady."

"Then why was she out riding in the middle of the night?"

"No one knows. It was so unlike her. A thorough investigation was done, and for a time we all thought the answer would be in Caroline's diary, for the child wrote in one every day, but no one could find it."

Lucy gaped. "It *disappeared*?"

"No, no. We just couldn't find it. It must be somewhere, I mean, who would take it?"

"Someone with an eye to murder, that's who," Lucy said grimly.

"Well, it wasn't a murder, so you can keep those thoughts to yourself," Verity replied testily. "The family was traumatized enough without such nonsense. I'm just hoping things are better now. Which is why we're here. My brother and his wife are in London visiting their son John, who is a captain in the Navy and has been temporarily brought to dock while awaiting repairs on his ship. So I'm to chaperone Charlotte until their return."

"It's quite kind of you to do so, my lady, but I still think—"

"Then stop. We are here to help, not make things worse by blathering about murders and what not, and all with no proof, mind you. No one would have wished harm upon Caroline. Everyone loved her."

"She seems a paragon. Does Miss Charlotte look like her sister?"

"Oh no, not at all. Although they are twins, they are as—I'm sorry—they *were* as different as day and night. Caroline looked just like my sister-in-law Olivia, blonde with silver gray eyes, and just as lovely and proper. Meanwhile, Charlotte has my brother Jack's coloring, auburn hair and deep blue eyes. She has . . ." Verity pursed her lips thoughtfully, searching for the right word. "Charlotte has *character*."

"Character?" Lucy looked unconvinced. "What does that mean?"

"It means she has a great deal of spirit and far too much intelligence for a girl her age." Verity hesitated, and then added, "She's not perfect, of course. There are . . . *things* that aren't quite as they should be with Charlotte."

"What do you mean by that?" The maid leaned closer. "My lady, is something wrong with Miss Charlotte?"

"No, of course not! There's nothing wrong with Charlotte! She just fine as she is. It's just that Caroline was always so perfect, at least by society's standards, that poor Charlotte was forever being compared to her sister, which was massively unfair."

"By society's standards, eh?" Lucy's thick brows rose. "But not by yours, my lady?"

"Never by mine. Charlotte was always my favorite. She has a restless soul, never lets her problems keep her from accomplishing things, and is always searching for . . . well, I don't know what. But something. Of course, that was before her sister passed." Verity stared out the window at the approaching house, a weight on her heart. "Her mother says Charlotte is quite different now. She's settled down and is even engaged to be married."

"That's good news, isn't it?"

"I suppose so," Verity said without conviction. "She's marrying a viscount. He's been a friend of the family for quite some time. He's the grandson of a local landowner, and is quite handsome, well bred, and very plump in the pocket."

Lucy nodded her approval. "A love match, then."

Verity didn't answer. To be honest, the engagement was the reason she'd accepted Olivia's request for assistance. Verity usually found the responsibilities of serving as chaperone too taxing, and would make excuses to avoid the task. But the news of Charlotte's engagement within months of her sister's death had been unsettling.

Verity rarely questioned her brother's and sister-in-law's judgement, for they were loving and kind parents. But she feared that Olivia and Jack were too bruised from Caroline's death to see what was occurring with their remaining daughter. Charlotte had experienced more than enough pain as it was, and Verity wasn't about to let her favorite niece make a mistake that might bring her yet more grief.

The coach rolled to a stop in front of the Hall. A footman leapt down to open the door and put the stepstool in place. Verity drew her cloak closer, turned her panniers so that they would fit through the door, and then stepped down onto the drive. A faint wind fluffed her skirts while her boots crunched upon the gravel. Behind her, Lucy gave instructions to the footmen about the many trunks tied to the back of the coach.

Verity eyed the house before her. The mist, oddly enough

much thicker now even with the sun well overhead, rolled over their boots like waves, breaking against Nimway's silvered walls and then dissipating into the damp air.

Lucy came to stand beside Verity, her thin nose almost quivering as she looked around. "There's an odd feeling to this place," she announced. "I can see why the locals tell tales. It *feels* enchanted."

"La, how you go on! It's not enchanted, and you'd be wise to remember that. Now come, let's find my niece and—"

The door to the great house opened.

Verity stepped forward in expectation, but no auburn-haired young lady came flying out to greet her. Instead, a tall, pinch-faced servant padded into the courtyard. He bowed as soon as he reached them. "Lady Barton, how are you? We've been expecting you."

"Thank you, Simmons." She looked over his shoulder at the open, empty doorway. "Where's Miss Charlotte?"

His thin lips folded in displeasure. "I fear she is out riding. She's been gone a few hours now and I'm not certain when she'll return."

"Heavens! Should we send someone to look for her?"

"I'm sure she's fine. She rides every morning and mentioned she might stop by the vicar's house and leave some flowers. I daresay the vicar's wife invited her to stay for lunch."

"Playing Lady of the Manor while her mother's gone, is she? Well, good for her."

Simmons didn't look as if he agreed. Indeed, he looked more as if he'd just swallowed a lemon, but after a moment of pained-faced struggle, he gave a short, polite nod.

Verity laughed. "Enough of your doom and gloom, Simmons! I've just spent hours in a coach and I haven't the stomach for it."

Simmons's mouth twitched, and a faint smile slipped out. "Yes, my lady. May I say that it will do Miss Charlotte good to have a visitor? It will do us *all* good."

"It will do me some good, too, for I'm quite fagged to death from attending balls and dinners and soirees. If I do not see another glass of orgeat until next year, it would please me greatly. I—Oh dear. I haven't yet introduced you to my new maid. Simmons, this is Lucy Hull. She'll need to know which rooms are ours so she can direct the delivery of the luggage."

"Of course, my lady. Miss Hull, welcome to Nimway Hall." He gestured to a nearby footman, who dashed up and, bowing, escorted Lucy toward the growing pile of luggage. Simmons turned back to Verity. "Lady Barton, I hope you don't mind, but when I saw your coach pulling up, I took the liberty to have a tea tray prepared and delivered to your bed chamber. I assume you still take a daily nap?"

"Why yes, I do. Thank you for remembering. You know how I enjoy my naps."

The butler's smile softened. "That I do, my lady."

"Good. Now come, let's get out of this damp air. It's making my curls sag, and that I cannot stand. Besides, I should at least find a comfortable chair while I'm waiting on Charlotte's return."

Still smiling, Simmons bowed and led the way inside.

CHAPTER 2

"*Mannaggia la miseria!* We are lost." The servant, an elderly man with a shock of white hair and sun-browned skin, eyed the surrounding trees as if offended by their very existence.

"I said as much an hour ago," Marco di Rossi answered shortly. "But you'd hear none of it. In fact, we've passed that tree three times now."

"Three times?" Pietro Luca, a master stonemason and an impossible assistant, cocked a disbelieving eye at the tree. "*Impossibile!*"

Marco's black gelding snorted his disgust. Marco patted the horse's neck and murmured, "You are right, Diavolo. He is stubborn like an old mule and will not listen to anyone."

"I should have ridden with the cart to Nimway Hall," Pietro muttered.

"I suggested that, too, but again you would have none of it," Marco said shortly. As irked as it made him, he never took Pietro's grumbling to heart. The stonemason was an old man, his hair so white it gleamed even in the shadow of the trees. No one knew his real age, including Pietro, although he claimed to be over ninety.

Marco, having witnessed the old man's strength and his indefatigable love of women, thought it closer to sixty.

However old he was, Pietro had one allegiance and that was to the di Marco family, which had rescued the Luca family from poverty and given them decades of employment in a variety of tasks. Pietro, who'd been just a youth when his grandfather had become head groomsman for the famous di Rossi stables, had been taught the valuable art of stonemasonry and had shown such a talent for selecting quality blocks of Carrara marble that by the time he was thirty, he'd become the master stonemason for the house.

From a young age, Marco had taken Pietro's knowledge of stone and turned it into art. And thus the perfect partnership had been born.

Pietro sniffed loudly. "The post boy at the inn lied. There is no shortcut. He's probably even now laughing at me. Why I should hunt him down like the dog he is and slit his throat for—"

"*Boh!* You waste your time with that halfwit. We must find Nimway Hall. The cart will already be there, and those fools cannot set up my workshop without instruction." The cart had gone ahead with two of Pietro's assistants, brawny lads brought to handle the large marble slabs Marco had brought with him. As soon as the marble was unloaded, they'd return to Italy and leave him and Pietro on site to finish the assignment.

Assignment. Curse is more like. He hadn't wanted to accept the overly generous offer from Mrs. Harrington to carve a 'unique to my home' marble fireplace to serve as a centerpiece for her dining room. But Marco's father, who'd once been a famous painter in his own right, had pointed out that the English market was ready for a favorite Italian sculptor and it would be foolish to turn down an assignment from someone so well connected. Marco couldn't disagree, especially after Mrs. Harrington casually mentioned that she couldn't wait to share her new treasure with the Queen, with whom she had more than a passing acquaintance.

It was one thing to sell one's work for mere money. But a recommendation to royalty? Ah . . . that was something else. And as the family fortune now rested solely on Marco's shoulders, he found that he couldn't say no.

He stifled a sigh and looked at the sun where it shone through the trees. At least the heavy mist was gone. That was helpful as it made the wood seem less . . . active. Marco grimaced at his own imagination. It was a normal wood, this. Slightly confusing, true, with its inclines and rambling pathways that all looked alike, but it was nothing more than that.

An owl hooted as if in defiance of his thoughts.

Pietro started, and his horse pranced nervously. The horse, a fat but small piebald the stonecutter fondly called 'Goliath' after the animal's unusually huge appetite, looked as if he was ready to bolt.

But then so did his rider. "Why is that owl awake at this time of the day?" Pietro asked loudly, suspicion in his voice.

"Perhaps we woke him, tromping under his perch over and over." Marco stared at the tree from where the hooting had come. Odd, he remembered all of the trees in this clearing except that gnarled oak. The tree was twisted and turned as if it had fought untold elements, its leaves fluttering in the wind as if trying to shake off a bad thought. On impulse, Marco turned Diavolo toward the crooked tree and rode past it, the owl hooting softly as they went. "Come, Pietro."

Grumbling, the stonemason followed, Goliath snorting nervously. They pushed through some shrubs and the path appeared before them.

Marco pulled up Diavolo and grinned. "Look! We've found the path again."

"We found *a* path," Pietro said in a flat tone. "I can only hope it's the right one."

"It is. I recognize that boulder."

Pietro looked at the large rock. His eyes flew wide and he made the sign of the cross. "That looks like a screaming spirit."

"It does not," Marco said sharply, although privately he thought Pietro was right; the boulder did look a little like a screaming face. But only a little.

Still, it was more than enough for Pietro, who said in a dark tone, "There's evil at work here."

Marco chuckled. "You are ridiculous. What do you think will happen? The angel of death will jump out of the woods and eat you—"

A white mare burst onto the path before them, scattering leaves and twigs. A girl – for she could be no more than sixteen, if that – sat astride the huge horse, the voluminous skirts of her sapphire blue habit flowing about her. Diavolo shied wildly. For a moment Marco held the animal in check, but somehow that damned knobby tree, which Marco had thought well behind him, managed to get in the way. His cloak tangled with some low hung branches and ensnared him.

He was more than a match for one or the other – the bolting horse or tangling with the low branches – but not both. The horse reared and, caught by the branches, he was thrown to the ground, his cloak ripping on a tree limb.

He landed on his back with a hard thud. Moments passed and all he could do was stare up at the flecks of blue sky visible between knotted branches, and fight for breath.

It was then it happened – an apparition blocked his view of the tree tops, one as vivid as it was surprising, a heart-shaped face surrounded by tousled dark red hair entangled with leaves, and freshly pinkened cheeks that contrasted with the bluest eyes he'd ever seen.

She was older than he'd thought, although not by much. If she was over twenty years of age, he'd have been surprised, and she was every bit as taking up close as she had been from a distance. The woman obviously didn't fear the sun, which became her greatly and added a faintly exotic air to what was already a fascinating collection of features. She reminded him of a painting he'd once seen in Naples of Venus arising from the sea, her long auburn tresses entwined with seaweed instead of leaves.

"Are you injured?" Her voice was low and musical, as comely as the rest of her.

Am I injured? He couldn't breathe well, and now he was seeing visions in blue.

"I should call for help." She started to rise.

He caught her wrist. The second his fingers touched her bare skin, a surge of pure, blazing fire ripped through him. His senses roared to life and all the air he'd thought he'd lost came racing back, filling his lungs and making him gasp at the shock.

She must have felt something as well, for she flushed and then yanked her wrist free, cradling it as if it were burned, her eyes wide, her lips parted.

He sat upright, his path as clear as if someone had whispered it into his ear. He leaned forward at the same time she did, and their lips met. It was almost as if someone had placed a hand on the back of each of their heads and gently led them together. They kissed, meeting with a furiously hot-blooded passion that roared like a wild fire racing through a too-dry forest. Oddly, there was none of the awkwardness of a first kiss. Instead, they kissed deeply as if they'd kissed a million times before, his hands buried in her silky hair as she clutched his coat, straining toward each other, desperate for more even as they consumed one another.

Her mount snorted noisily, breaking the moment. Their gazes locked and they froze, staring at one another, startled and shocked.

The woman gasped, her breath sweet on his lips before she scrambled to her feet. "We—I—" Hand pressed to her mouth, she whirled around and went to her horse, lurching a bit in her hurry. Once there, she clung to the saddle as it was the only thing holding her upright. "We—That was—" She shook her head as if trying to clear her thoughts.

She looked as bemused as he felt. She had a fascinating face, this bewildering woman who'd kissed him with such burning passion but now wouldn't even meet his gaze. His first impression had been right; she was beautiful, although not in the traditional sense of bland symmetry. Her beauty was more piquant, and less classical in natural. Her face was heart-shaped, but her nose bold and her jaw firm. Her sun-kissed skin was intriguingly marked by a scatter of freckles, while her deep blue eyes were fringed with long, thick lashes that gave her a slightly impish look.

Marco climbed to his feet, slightly stung by his bruised pride. It had been years – almost decades – since he'd been thrown from a horse in such a humiliating manner. Although, truth be told, that damned kiss had offset him far more than being thrown to the ground. *Dio, what a kiss.* He was still dizzy from it, which was incomprehensible. *What in the hell just happened?*

Overhead, as if in approval, the owl hooted, and drew the woman's bemused glance.

Marco read her curious expression and explained, "We woke him when we rode under his tree."

The woman's gaze flickered to the woods behind him, her brows arching. "We?"

Marco looked around but saw only Diavolo standing a few yards away, stomping the ground to express his displeasure. Pietro and his grumpy mount were gone. *That fool.* Marco bit back an irritated sigh. "My assistant was here. He seems to have left in the madness." It was more likely that Goliath had left, and had taken Pietro with him, but Marco didn't feel like explaining.

He turned back to the woman and allowed himself a smile. "Of course, were he here, then that kiss wouldn't have—"

"There was no kiss," she said sharply.

His smile slipped. "What?"

"There was no kiss." Her gaze pinned him in place, not giving an inch.

Why would anyone – this woman, much less – want to deny what had been so pleasurable? "Say what you will, but I know what I know," he returned. "I was there, too, and I can still taste it."

Her cheeks deepened in color. "I don't know what you're talking about."

She looked so proud, her chin in the air, her mouth set in a mulish line, that his irritation slowly vanished, and was quickly replaced with amusement. *Why not?* he decided. *Perhaps she is right, and that is a safer road for us both.* He shrugged. "Fine. If that is what you wish, then there was no kiss."

"I don't even know how we—But no." She shook her head. "It should never have happened."

Marco removed a leaf from his sleeve. "What should never have happened?" he teased.

Her lips quirked, as if she fought a smile. Satisfied, he went to collect Diavolo. He checked the horse's legs for injuries, glad to see there were none.

Her voice, husky yet clear, broke the silence. "That's a beautiful horse."

"Thank you. I trained Diavolo myself." Marco led his mount back to the path.

"He is bold, that one. I can see it in his eyes."

Diavolo arched his neck as if to agree, and Marco silently consigned his animal to the devil he'd been named after. As much as Marco wished it otherwise, the woman's rich voice reminded him of red wine, delicious and heady. And when he'd held her in his arms, her mouth open under his, she'd been every bit as intoxicating.

His body warmed at the memory and, realizing her gaze rested on his face, he tried to redirect his thoughts from that kiss, but failed. *Good God, I cannot stop thinking about it. What's wrong with me? Did I injure my head in the fall?* He ran his hand through his hair, searching for a tell-tale knot that might explain this instant, heated attraction, but found none.

He realized she was watching him with a concerned expression, so he dropped his hand to his side. Her horse whinnied, baring its teeth and then favoring him with a caustic look. "Your horse appears to be as opinionated as mine."

The woman fondly patted the animal's neck. "You have no idea. Her name is Angelica, but my father says a better name would be 'Obstinate.'" The horse nuzzled her owner, before it turned its accusing stare back on Marco.

"She is angry with me."

"She's protective." The woman's gaze narrowed. "Your accent . . . You're Italian."

He nodded.

"Ah! You're the sculptor. I wouldn't have thought that."

The disbelief in her tone irked him. "I am Marco di Rossi. And you are?"

"Charlotte Harrington. My mother said a sculptor was coming from Italy and, as she had to leave, I was to make sure you received her instructions. She left you a letter."

"She is not here?"

"She was called to London. The head groom is to see to it that you have everything you need."

"I won't need much. I brought everything with me. The wagon carrying the marble and my tools should have arrived earlier this morning."

"I should have known who you were from your accent, but I didn't think a sculptor would look—" Miss Harrington caught herself and grimaced. "No. Never mind."

He was amused despite himself. "What did you think a sculptor would look like?"

"Well, not like—" She bit her lip. "It's just that you're dressed so . . ." Her gaze traveled over him, touching on the square cut emerald pin set in his cravat, the silk waistcoat embroidered in silver, and the expensive lace that fell over his wrists. "You're so *fancy*," she blurted out.

He choked back an impolite word. *Fancy?* What in the hell? "I beg your pardon?" he said stiffly. "Surely even a sculptor may dress as he wishes."

"Of course you may," Miss Harrington said hastily, her brow creased as she continued to stare at him the same way he imagined she might watch a dancing monkey. "I've met only a few artists," she confessed, "and none dressed as fashionably as you." Her gaze dropped to his cuffs, and she added in a somber tone, "It would be sad to see such lace dirtied."

"I don't wear this when I work," he retorted.

"Good, although, if you wanted to, I suppose you could tuck your cuffs up and wear an apron of some sort, or even—" She caught his expression and had the grace to flush. "I'm sorry. I shouldn't be speaking. I don't know anything about sculpting."

"So I've noticed," he returned in a dry tone, although his irritation had softened at her honesty. The sunlight filtered through the trees above and shimmered in odd patterns over her hair and face.

He curled his fingers against the desire to reach into his saddlebag for paper and charcoal, as everything about her invited him to capture her likeness. Even more interesting than her features was the hint of sadness to her mouth, a tragedy unspoken. Was he imagining that? he wondered.

Defiant and intriguing, she teased his senses. And every second he spent in her presence, his desire grew. Unaware of his hungry regard, Miss Harrington led her horse a few steps to where a tree had fallen, sticks crackling under her boots.

"You're limping." He hadn't seen her fall, but something must have occurred.

"I'm fine." She stepped onto the tree trunk and, with the expediency of long experience, swung back into the saddle with a lithe move and adjusted her skirts. "What were you and your servant doing on this path? You were going the wrong direction if you wished to go to Nimway."

"We were lost. When you came upon us, we'd just found the pathway again."

"Balesboro Wood does such things," she said.

He raised his brows. "You speak as if the forest was alive."

"My sister used to say Balesboro picks its favorites, helping them through, while trapping those it does not like."

"Your sister is very fanciful, then."

Something flickered in the deep blue eyes. A flash so dark that Marco's own heart staggered from the strength of it. *What's that?*

Whatever it was, Miss Harrington quickly hid it. "It's this way to the Hall." Without waiting for an answer, she turned her horse down the path and left him alone with Diavolo.

He swung himself back into the saddle and urged his horse after her. They quickly caught up, and he fell in behind her on the narrow path. "What of my servant? I don't know where he is."

She answered over her shoulder, her profile in bold relief against the leafy green trees. "We'll send one of the grooms to fetch him. They know Balesboro well." She turned back, indicating there was no need for more conversation.

Marco was left riding behind her, admiring the ease with which she handled her huge mare.

The silence lengthened, and Marco grew impatient. Yet his very real irritation was tinged with a growing curiosity. From the time he'd been old enough to notice them, women had favored him, especially once he'd gained some fame as a sculptor. Yet this woman seemed almost anxious to be rid of him, and that was despite their burning kiss. In fact, as the moments slid by, Miss Charlotte Harrington seemed to have forgotten he was even here.

He scowled at the woods where the leaves quivered as if laughing at him. "Do we have much longer to go?"

She didn't even bother to turn. "No."

He noticed that the wood wasn't as thick now, and the sun

shone through much more. A beam of light rested on Miss Harrington's hair, gold threads appearing, twined among the auburn curls. He remembered the heavy silk of her hair when he'd sunk his hands into it during their kiss. If he curled his fingers closed, he could almost feel the weight of it now.

Diavolo looked back at Marco and snorted, as if in laughter. "Stop that." Marco muttered to the ornery horse.

The gelding shook his head and yanked on the reins.

"Keep that up and you'll never see another apple so long as you live," Marco told him.

Miss Harrington sent him a surprised look over her shoulder. "What's that?"

"I'm sorry. I was talking to my horse."

Her lips curved. "I talk to Angelica, too."

"So long as she doesn't talk back, no one can take issue with it."

A deep chuckle escaped Miss Harrington and he found himself yearning for another. To his relief, the path widened and he moved Diavolo up to ride beside her. "I owe you an apology."

She flushed. "You don't need to apologize for the kiss. I was as much a part of it as you."

"What kiss?"

Her lips quirked, but she managed to hide her smile.

"I owe you an apology for not looking the way you imagined a sculptor should. With your mother gone, you are my sponsor and I should not disappoint you in such a way."

Her eyes warmed with amusement. "I was disappointed," she admitted.

"Of course. You thought I should have been covered in dust and wearing a dirty smock and a – how do you say it? – *berretto?*"

"A ber-Oh, you mean a cap. No, no." She sniffed loftily. "I expected nothing so silly."

But her tone of voice belied her words, so he said, "I hope you will share the history of your home so that I might design something suitable enough to win your mother's approval. If you do, I might be prevailed upon to wear a cap for you."

Miss Harrington smiled. "I will hold you to that, although it's only fair to warn you that my mother can be very particular." She turned her attention back to the pathway. "Perhaps it's best my mother's not here."

He'd already decided that much was true, for he found the daughter quite intriguing. Perhaps, if he won her trust, he could convince her to sit for him and let him sketch her. *There are so many things I could do with those features. They intrigue me as few have.*

How would he render her likeness, he wondered? Perhaps as a Greek handmaiden wearing a draped gown, one shoulder bared, a jug of water in her graceful hands. But . . . no. Not as a handmaiden. She wasn't bland enough for such a trite depiction. Her features deserved something unique. But what? A goddess, perhaps? Oh yes. That held possibilities. She would be a ripe, sensual goddess of the earth with leaves tangled in her curls, her curves echoing the roll of the mountains, her bold nose and forthright stare daring the observer to—

"We turn here." She guided her horse onto a wider path, this one graveled and smooth.

Marco reluctantly released his creative imagery and focused on where he was. "We are close to the house?"

"It is only a few minutes away." She kept her eyes fastened ahead. "I hope the accommodations my mother arranged will be satisfactory."

"I do not need much. I brought my tools and slabs of marble. I asked only that my workshop have ample room and plenty of sunlight."

"Then the old stables will make an excellent workshop. But I was thinking more of your housing. Mama thought the stables would be spacious enough and that you and your servant could sleep in the rooms the grooms once used, but now that I see you . .

." She cast a quick glance his way, eyeing his clothes again. "You cannot sleep in the stables."

"I must sleep near the marble. I work when the mood strikes and sometimes it strikes at three in the morning." He shrugged. "I never know when, but I must be near the stone when it happens."

"That must be very inconvenient for your wife."

"I'm not married."

"Oh." She rode in silence for a moment. "You live alone, then."

"I am rarely alone. I have many brothers and sisters, and we live within steps of one another. In fact, they and their families are often at my house."

She looked away, and he was instantly alert. *What has caused that sadness, he wondered.*

She turned back, the shadow he'd seen was gone.

He expected her to let the subject drop, but she asked in a wistful tone, "How many brothers and sisters do you have?"

"I am the middle child of seven."

Her brows rose. "*Seven?*"

"Most of them have children and wives or husbands, too." He considered this a moment. "I'm not sure why they like to gather at my house, because it's not the largest, but that is how it is."

"That sounds lovely."

"It is a little like living in an army camp, with large meals and far too much activity."

She slanted him a curious look. "If they are always at your house, how do you find the quiet to work?"

"I lock the door."

"Ah. Efficient."

He grinned. "And necessarily direct. My father is a well-known painter, Vicento di Rossi."

"Oh! I've heard of him."

Marco nodded. "Most people have. When I was growing up, my father often worked from home. We all knew to leave him alone when his workshop door was closed, but if the door was open . . . ah, that was different. Then he was with us, telling tales about princes and popes, maidens and saints. There was much to learn, and much he taught us."

"How *lovely*." Her voice lowered as if in reverence.

"How *noisy*."

Miss Harrington laughed, the sound as husky and inviting as he'd imagined. "You will have plenty of quiet at Nimway. It is very peaceful here and—Ah! There's the house now."

The Hall appeared before them, sitting on a bluff and surrounded by the sweep of a green lawn. He noted with admiration the use of local stone and the simple, but powerful lines. "It is beautiful."

"It's Nimway," she said simply. She'd pulled to a stop where the path split, and he joined her. Her gaze fastened on an ornate carriage that sat before the front doors. "My aunt has arrived and will be wondering where I am."

And now I am dismissed. "Of course," he said, although he had to fight a surge of disappointment. "Where are the stables?"

She turned back to him, framed by the green lawn and the darker forest beyond.

Dio, but I want a painting of her, of this moment.

"That path will take you to the stables. Richardson is the head groom and will be expecting you. He can send someone to find your lost servant."

That was that, then. From now on, Marco would only see her in passing, or for a few minutes here and there when she came to inspect his work. *Which is how it should be,* he told himself firmly.

And yet, he found himself lingering. "I'm glad we met." The words escaped him before he could stop them, and he silently cursed his lack of finesse. She was like a deer, this one, and one bold move could send her bolting.

Her gaze darkened, and she increased the emptiness between them with distant politeness. "Thank you. My mother wished me to impress upon you how important it is that you finish on time."

"In four weeks. She was very firm about the schedule in our correspondence."

"Good. I'm to make sure you have everything you want—" Her face colored and she added hastily, "No, not everything you *want*. I meant to say I'm to make sure you have everything you *need* for your work. I didn't mean—"

"I know what you meant. Do not worry. I will let you know if there's anything I need *or* want." Smiling, he inclined his head. "And I'm sure there will be."

"Mr. di Rossi, I don't mean to—"

"Please, call me Marco."

Her face pinkened. "I shouldn't—"

"Ah, but you will," he said firmly. "Now go, your aunt awaits. We will speak again soon." With that, he turned Diavolo toward the stable, aware that she stayed where she was, watching him ride away.

CHAPTER 3

Lucy removed another gown from the trunk, pausing to unwrap the protective tissue paper from the delicate silk. "I don't know why you brought so many ball gowns. We'll only be here for a few weeks and except for the wedding, there are no formal events."

Verity, who was peering out the window, answered in an absent tone, "I know, but now I'll have a variety of choices for the wedding day, which is good, for I have no idea what colors Olivia will wear, and I cannot clash with my own sister-in-law or—Oh!" She straightened. "There's Charlotte, returning from her ride now."

"It's about time," Lucy said. "We've been here two hours already."

"Yes, and—" Verity's eyes widened. "Oh, my."

Lucy paused in hanging yet another gown. "What is it, my lady?"

"Did we pack my opera glasses? They would be most useful."

"I don't believe so."

"A pity. It's difficult to tell from this distance, but her companion looks to be very handsome—"

Lucy was already peering over Verity's shoulder. "He does, indeed. Is that the Viscount?"

"No, he is slender of frame. Personally, I prefer a man with shoulders like – well, like that one." *My dear Charlotte, where did you find that treasure?* Perhaps Nimway Hall wasn't as secluded as Verity thought.

Lucy agreed. "Broad-shouldered men are handsomer. Take Lord Rackingham, for example."

Verity had done just that, and on more than one occasion, but all she said was, "I wonder who this gentleman might be? His clothing is quite fine, and—Oh! He has left her and is riding down the path to the stables."

"He must be one of those gentlemen who like to oversee the care of their own horses. Gentlemen who enjoy hunting often do such things."

"I suppose so," Verity said. "Perhaps it's best he won't be with Charlotte when I see her. That way I can ask about him."

Charlotte was now approaching the house, her horse clipping along at a smooth trot.

"What a monstrous huge animal," Lucy said in a critical tone. "No lady ride should ride such a brute."

"The mare is large, but while she's a handful with others, she's quite gentle with Charlotte." Or so Verity's brother Jack had insisted when she'd said something similar.

A groom hurried forward to hold Charlotte's horse as she dismounted. She looked at the coach as she unpinned her hat and tucked it under arm, speaking for a few moments with the groom before she came inside.

"Oh no, the poor thing is limping!" Lucy frowned. "That big horse must have thrown her—"

"She always limps," Verity said shortly, snapping the curtain to. "But not overtly so. In fact, she limps a *very* little, and even then, she does it *gracefully*."

"She limps *gracefully*? How can anyone—" Verity's expression froze the maid's words in place. After a moment, Lucy cleared her throat. "I'm sorry, my lady. I wasn't thinking."

"No, you weren't. I will tell you this, but only because I know that if I don't, you'll go asking embarrassing questions in the servants' quarters. My niece's back isn't as straight as it could be, but she's perfectly fine as she is, and there's no need to say another word about it."

"Oh dear. Such a pity, my lady. Has Miss Charlotte always been like that?"

"It began when she was only ten and grew worse every year until she was fifteen, when it stopped. It was a great relief for us all, but especially to Charlotte, for it sent that wretched horde of doctors with their tortuous cures away once and for all."

"One of the must have worked."

"I doubt it. I think it stopped because she was no longer growing. If you knew what that child has been through – painful braces and weights and some contraption where she was suspended from her shoulders for hours— Oh dear! When I think about it now, it sickens me. It was quite unfair, although at the time, there seemed to be no choice. We all wanted her to heal. Thankfully, nothing worse seems to have come of it other than a slightly curved back and a small limp. A small price, considering everything."

Lucy tsked. "Poor Miss Charlotte. So pretty, and to be a crippl—"

"*What?* You *wretch!*"

Lucy fell back a step. "My lady?"

"Don't you *ever* say that word again! Do you hear me?"

"I—I—I'm sorry. I—I didn't mean—"

"Not another word! I'm leaving. I am going to visit my lovely and *perfect* niece." Verity yanked her shawl from where she'd dropped it on a chair earlier, tossed it about her shoulders, and swept to the door. "You, meanwhile, will stay here and finish unpacking!"

Without waiting for an answer, Verity slammed the door behind her. In stiff outrage, she marched down the hallway. When she reached the stairwell, she stopped and leaned against the wall, her heart thudding sickly. She shouldn't have lost her temper, but oh, how she hated the heavy-handed term Lucy had flung about as if that cold and cruel word didn't weigh a thing.

Verity might not have children of her own, but her feelings for her nieces and nephew had made her all too aware of both the joys and the pains of being a parent. She'd witnessed Charlotte's struggles far too long, and far too intimately, not to feel them herself.

Unwilling to let her niece see her so upset, which would easily raise questions Verity had no intention of answering, she attempted to calm herself, pacing back and forth across the hallway, eventually recovering herself enough to admire the lovely new rugs and silk wallpaper.

Calmed, Verity smoothed her hair, adjusted her shawl, and then continued downstairs where she found Charlotte in the great hall speaking with Simmons.

"Aunt Verity!" Charlotte's smile instantly banished Verity's dark mood. "I was on my way to see you!" She left the butler and hurried forward, her riding boots muffled by the thick rugs.

The last time Verity had seen her niece, she'd been dressed in a faded, worn riding habit, one cuff torn loose, her hair tangled with twigs, her cheeks flushed from a wild ride she'd just taken through the fields surrounding Nimway. It was hard to reconcile that image with the one Verity faced now. Gone was the woefully out of date riding habit. Now Charlotte was dressed in a fashionable brushed wool riding habit of sapphire blue, her hair coiffed in a current style, a beautiful fall of lace spilling from the neck. Except for her slightly sun-darkened skin, she could easily have been any of a number of young women of fashion.

But as she drew closer, Verity realized that a few of Charlotte's auburn curls had come loose from their pins and lay tangled on her shoulder, while grass clung to her skirt beside a stain near her knee.

Verity breathed a sigh of relief. *There's still some of the old Charlotte left. Thank God for that.* She held out her arms. "Charlotte, my dear, how *are* you?"

Charlotte sank into her aunt's perfumed hug with a laugh. Oh, how she loved her Aunt Verity; no one made Charlotte laugh more. "I was beginning to think you weren't coming. Mama was certain you'd arrive last Tuesday."

"Your Mama was ever the optimist, but even she must have known I could not miss the Duchess of Richmond's ball. It was a costumed affair, and you know how I love those."

Charlotte smiled. When she was a child, one of her favorite past times had been going through her aunt's closet, as it had been stuffed with glittering gowns and elaborate costumes. "Did you wear that lovely swan mask you showed me the last time I visited?"

"Oh no. I wore the swan costume to a masquerade at a private dinner at Vauxhall for the Earl of Cragnair two seasons ago. When one is in society, one cannot wear the same costume twice. That would be gauche."

"So what did you wear to the Richmond ball?"

"I dressed in a silver gown and went as Venus. It was risqué but tasteful. My new maid Lucy put my hair up in such a way, what with silver ribbands and bows and little arrows and – well, it was perfection. No one could say enough about it." Aunt Verity, who always looked as if she were half asleep, flashed her easy smile, although today her eyes seemed unusually bright.

"I'll wager you were the loveliest one there."

"I believe you're right," Aunt Verity agreed with a sweet smile. "I looked quite exceptional. After all, silver is my color."

Simmons, who'd been waiting a respectful distance away, now cleared his throat. "Forgive me for intruding, but although Lady

Barton had tea when she first arrived, I wonder if she'd enjoy another cup? It is a bit damp today."

"Lud, yes," Aunt Verity said fervently.

The butler smiled. "I'll make certain you have extra sugar for your tea, as well."

Aunt Verity couldn't have looked more pleased. "Simmons, you must come and work for me at Chase Manor."

Charlotte gasped with laughter. "Aunt Verity! You shouldn't attempt to steal Mama's butler!"

"All is fair in love and servants. Your Mama would be the first to agree."

The butler bowed, looking pleased. "I'm honored, but I cannot accept your kind offer. Mr. Harrington would never allow it."

Aunt Verity made a face. "My brother can be so infuriating. I suppose I shall have to make do with inept Rochester. He can barely hear, you know, and is cross as a bear."

Charlotte shook her head. "Rochester loves you and you would be sad if he were not there to greet you when you got home."

"He would be perfectly happy to retire, should I find a replacement of Simmons' equal."

The butler almost preened. "I do what I can, my lady. Now, if you'll excuse me, I'll fetch tea." He bowed and left.

Aunt Verity sighed. "Such a treasure." Her gaze returned to Charlotte. "But look at you! You look radiant, my dear, although I do wish you'd stay out of the sun. You're getting quite dark, and that will never do."

Charlotte chuckled. "Now you sound just like Mama."

"Your Mama is a woman of great sense and, I must say, has shown an exceptional talent for decorating." Verity gestured around the great hall where two new chandeliers, freshly uphol-stered furniture, and numerous gold framed paintings were on display. "So many changes! I almost didn't recognize it."

That was an exaggeration, Charlotte decided. Even with the new decorations, the great hall was a still very much a relic of time past. With its heavy dark mahogany paneling and the huge, medieval style fireplace in the far wall, accented by heavy oak beams that spanned the entire width of the room, the great hall still whispered of times gone by. In fact, if she closed her eyes, she could imagine kings and queens holding court before the fireplace, knights in shining armor eyeing a bevy of beautifully gowned ladies-in-waiting.

Even with many changes Mama had wrought on the hall, there was no way to completely eradicate the historic feel of the room. *I'm glad for that. This is the heart of the house and it shouldn't be changed.*

"Shall we repair to the sitting room?" Charlotte asked.

"Must you change out of your habit first?"

"And have to wait for all of the latest news from London? Heavens, no! I shall change after tea." She linked arms with her aunt and they walked to the sitting room.

As soon as they entered the room, Aunt Verity made her way to the settee closest to the fire and collapsed upon it, looking around the room with approval. "Your mother has done wonders with this room." She picked up a cream silk pillow and smoothed the blue tassel that hung from one corner. "I do love the neoclassical style."

"I warned you in my letter that Mama was redecorating the entire house." Or rather, expelling everything that wasn't nailed down. It wasn't that Charlotte didn't like the changes; they were beautiful and it was nice to see Nimway Hall get the love she deserved. It was more a feeling of being left behind, as if Mama was purging the house of everything Caroline had so much as looked at, including Charlotte.

She pushed the uncomfortable thought away and sat beside her aunt. "I'm so glad you came."

"I wouldn't have missed it for the world, although I hope your mama's desire to redecorate does not include loud men in dirty boots tromping in and out while hammering on things."

"Nothing so elaborate. Mainly new wallpaper, rugs, furniture, and curtains, although she has commissioned a new marble fireplace for the dining room. It's to be installed in the next few weeks." Charlotte tried to ignore an instant, heated memory of a pair of dark, chocolate-colored eyes, and a lop-sided smile that could charm a stone, and failed miserably.

"How lovely that will be." Aunt Verity propped her feet on a small stool, her skirts rustling in the quiet. "So tell me, my child, what tiresome tasks are we to oversee while I'm here? Your mother said something about a dressmaker?"

"I have fittings for my trousseau. Mama is worried it won't be ready in time."

"Ah yes. Your wedding." Aunt Verity's sleepy gaze rested on Charlotte's face. "It is soon, isn't it?"

"In a month." One month . . . *Goodness, that is so close.* Charlotte's heart sank and it took all of her efforts to keep her smile in place. "Mama is an uproar over the decorations for the chapel, the invitations for the wedding breakfast, the flowers for service, and – oh so many things."

"Which is good since Caroline—" Aunt Verity's lips quivered, her soft face folding as emotion overtook her.

"Aunt Verity, please don't cry!" Charlotte dug her kerchief out of her pocket, and handed it to her aunt. When Charlotte had been growing up, she'd refused to keep a handkerchief in her pocket. Mama had scolded, saying all ladies carried them, but Charlotte had resisted. Or she had until things had changed and tears had become as common place as the sun rising. Now Charlotte never left her room without her handkerchief.

Aunt Verity dabbed at her eyes. "I'm so sorry! I vowed not to mention her, and yet here I am. 'Tis sad, but I cannot be trusted with a delicate situation. It's against my nature."

"You are too much like me, saying what you think."

Aunt Verity placed her hand on her niece's knee. "It's a curse, isn't it?"

"A horrid one." Charlotte mustered a smile, even though her chest ached as if someone sat on it. She was getting quite good at that, at smiling when she didn't feel like it, and she wondered if she was now more mask than face.

Aware that her aunt watched, Charlotte added, "I worry about Mama. She misses Caroline dreadfully."

"I know," Aunt Verity said with a sigh. "How's my dear brother doing?"

"Papa's been busy cheering up Mama, which has helped him more than anything. They are getting better slowly. I don't know what they'd do without one another." Charlotte shook her head ruefully. "After all this time, they are still madly in love. They've set a bar none of us will ever rise to."

"I'm certain you'll attain their level of marital bliss. Or you will if you marry the right man." Aunt Verity gave Charlotte a direct look. "You *are* marrying the right man, aren't you?"

Goodness, why would Aunt Verity say such a thing? "Of course I am. I've known Viscount Ashbrook since I was a child. Why, John, Caroline, and I were practically raised with Robert here at Nimway and Mama believes he will be a calm, steady husband."

"I know Ashbrook, for he was always underfoot when you were growing up. I must say, though, I cringe at the concept of a calm, steady husband for someone with your spirit. You don't have the Harrington auburn hair because you're 'calm' and 'steady.' We suffer from wild passions that complicate our lives and can lead us to do thoughtless and at times reprehensible things. How would your calm, steady Robert handle that, I wonder?"

"Things have changed in the last year. *I've* changed. I'm not the scofflaw you think me. I'm a Harrington, true, and I have the auburn hair of one, and the temper, but I'm not the same as I once was."

Aunt Verity reached out to pluck a blade of grass that had tangled with the lace on Charlotte's skirt. "Really?"

"I was walking in the garden earlier," Charlotte lied as she tucked her feet under her skirts. She could only hope she'd gotten all the mud from her boots. It was possible that before her intriguing encounter in the woods with a lost sculptor, she'd visited her favorite spot beside the stream that cut through Balesboro Wood. There, away from the watchful eyes of the servants, she'd stripped off her boots and stockings, sat on a sun-warmed rock, and trailed her bare feet in the cool water. *So far, it's been a lovely day.*

Aunt Verity rolled her eyes. "Yes, yes, you're an angel of goodness."

Charlotte grinned. "At times."

"Ha! Stubborn, that's what you are. I vow, but you are so much like my brother that I could scream. Where is Ashbrook now?"

"He's in London at his cousin's house taking care of some business before the wedding." *I think.* To be honest, Charlotte only knew Robert was in London because she'd noted the postmark on the hasty note she'd received from him a month ago. The note had been no more than a two-line scrawl informing her that, once again, he was postponing his return to Nimway and how he knew she would understand and wouldn't mind. This time, he hadn't even bothered giving a reason.

She supposed that if she'd been doing the same thing as he (writing to tell someone for the fifth time in a row that she wasn't appearing as she'd promised) she wouldn't have bothered to give an excuse, either. She was disappointed and yet also strangely relieved, and it was that last feeling that bothered her the most. Shouldn't she *want* him to visit? They weren't in love, of course, and were too mature to pretend otherwise, but still they were engaged and that should have accorded her some sort of attention.

A soft knock heralded the arrival of Simmons and the tea tray.

While he fixed two cups, Charlotte wondered if she should write Robert again and instead of asking when he might return, demand it.

She took a tea cup from Simmons and hid her sigh behind it. Why should she have to demand Robert's return? He should want to be here, with her. Still, as irked and uncertain as his continuing absence made her, she couldn't accept that he didn't have a perfectly good reason. Robert had been a significant part of her life for years. As a child, and then later as a young man, he'd visited his grandmother nigh every summer, riding to nearby Nimway where he'd quickly become her brother John's best friend, the two inseparable. He'd visited so often, that Mama and Papa had eventually assigned him his own bedchamber.

When John left to fulfil his commission in the Navy, Charlotte and Caroline had expected to see less of Robert, but to their surprise he'd visited just as often. Those four summers had been glorious, filled with picnics, laughter-filled evenings playing cards or re-enacting scenes from the newest novels, and – for her, at least, as Caroline didn't enjoy riding the way Charlotte and Robert did – enthusiastic rides across the lands and fields of Nimway. Last year, when Charlotte and Caroline had been presented at court and had their short, rather calamitous season, Robert had been there, too, always ready to escort them and Mama to whatever amusement called.

Charlotte considered him a dear friend, but during the dark months after Caroline's death, he'd become more than that. It had been his gentleness and care during that horrible time that had led Charlotte to accept his sudden, unexpected proposal.

And now, they were to be married.

She couldn't quite get her mind around that fact. He'd left the second she'd said yes, claiming he had to "set things to rights" before they married. At the time, she'd applauded his common sense, but when he'd left nothing behind but a weak breadcrumb trail of sparse notes that were anything but reassuring, her doubts had grown. Now the uncertainty pressed upon her, a heavy boulder balanced on an already unsteady stack.

Something had changed, only she wasn't sure what. She hoped that once she and Robert spent some time together, that they'd return to their previous easy, comfortable relationship and her doubts would be banished.

However Charlotte felt, it wouldn't do to let Aunt Verity know. As much as Charlotte loved her aunt, everyone knew Verity couldn't keep a secret to save her life, and would immediately spill everything to Mama.

Simmons handed Aunt Verity her cup of tea, and then he picked up the empty tray and bowed his way from the room.

She sighed happily. "No one knows how I like my tea better than Simmons."

"He's quite good," Charlotte agreed.

Aunt Verity's sleepy gaze rested back on Charlotte. "I'm rather surprised the household isn't in more of a tizzy, what with a wedding in the offing."

"We're all in a tizzy, especially Mama. The wedding has kept her mind off other things. She's been despondent since Caroline —" The word stuck in Charlotte's throat and, just like that, deep soul-shattering sadness roared over her.

She'd discovered over the last year that grief wasn't a constant. It didn't reside within one's mind every minute, but was instead a stealthy thief, sneaking up from behind when one least expected it, and snatching away one's happiness in the blink of an eye. Then it would slip away again, hiding in wait, ready to return as soon as one's guard was down.

"Oh child!" Aunt Verity set down her cup and patted Charlotte's hand where it was balled on her knee in a fist. "Don't look like that. I'm so sorry for mentioning it – Lud, I'm ruining everything!"

"No, no. It's not you. Sometimes, it just hits me. I think I've wept my last tear, but there always seems to be another."

"Oh dear. I'm so, so sorry. Perhaps . . . Would it help if we talked about something else?"

Charlotte sent her aunt a grateful look. "Yes, please."

"I saw you riding in on that big, white brute of a horse. I take it you are still riding every day?"

"When I can, yes. I'd just returned from—" Charlotte froze, her words stuck in her throat. *Good God, did Aunt Verity see me talking with di Rossi?* Charlotte sent a searching glance at her aunt, but all she saw on Verity's round face was bland, polite enquiry. Relieved, Charlotte said, "I love to ride. With Mama gone, I've been able to do it more often."

"I'm glad you're getting some fresh air. It's good for you in so many ways—Why, look at the color in your cheeks now!"

Charlotte murmured her agreement and then hurried to change the topic, asking if Aunt Verity had heard any good gossip whilst she was in town.

That did the trick. Brightening, Aunt Verity instantly dived into all of the latest on-dits while Charlotte pretended interest.

There were many things Charlotte was willing to share with her beloved aunt, but the short time she'd spent in the wood with a sculptor, a meeting that had included a shocking kiss, was not one of them. Neither did she wish to share the particulars of her precious morning rides across the golden hills and fields of Nimway, around the sparkling waters of Myrrdin Lake, and through the twisty, mysterious paths of Balesboro Wood. Those belonged to her and no one else. Since she'd been a child, especially after the never-ending procession of doctors and physicians began to file through her home, she never felt more at peace than when she rode wild and unfettered. Or so it had been before Caroline had died. Since then, nothing made Charlotte feel whole. She felt lost. Adrift. And painfully lonely.

Aunt Verity shared a scandalous rumor about the prince and a certain Catholic widow. As the story progressed, her words slowed, and she often yawned, her eyes drooping, and Charlotte knew her aunt would soon be asleep.

While Charlotte waited, she glanced down at her hands, where the emerald and old gold engagement ring Robert had given her winked in the sunlight. She closed her fingers around the warm metal, her thoughts slipping from Robert and to a dark-haired man with a compelling gaze, his smoky laugh as delicious as honey.

She wanted – no, she *craved* – more of that, she realized with a sinking feeling. She wasn't sure if it was the illicit nature of the man himself, his dark Italian good looks, or his patent unsuitability, but just the thought of seeing him again made her heart quicken. Her aunt's words about the Harrington red hair and their propensity to break rules came tumbling back. If Charlotte wished her life to remain on the safe, prudent course she'd set since Caroline's death, she'd avoid men like that.

It was a surprisingly disappointing thought, but she knew she had no choice. She had to control her impulsive nature until Robert returned, and then everything would work out.

It will because it has to.

It wasn't much, but right now, with Robert absent, it was all Charlotte had.

CHAPTER 4

Three days later, Simmons walked into the breakfast room carrying a salver holding a neat stack of letters. "The post has arrived, miss."

"Thank you." Charlotte pushed back her plate, took the packet of letters, and sorted through them. There were a number of missives addressed to her aunt, one rather plain letter for her father from his solicitor, a fashion magazine for her mother, an invitation to tea from the vicar's wife, and a bill from the mantua maker.

Everything but a letter from Robert.

She dropped the letters back on the salver Simmons held, and tried not to let her disappointment show.

The butler's mouth thinned. "I take it Viscount Ashbrook has not written?"

She sighed. "No. I wish he would, because—" A thought caught her. "Simmons, I wrote the Viscount a letter two weeks ago. Perhaps it wasn't sent. That would explain why he hasn't written back."

"I put your letter to his lordship on the mail coach myself, miss, as I was in town that day. He should have received it last week."

"Of course. That's that, then." She managed a smile she was certain didn't look at all real. "Thank you. That will be all."

The butler cleared his throat, obviously dying to say something else.

She hated to ask. Because of the difficulties she'd faced as a child, the butler and the rest of the staff were far too protective of her, assuming she needed extra assistance when she was perfectly fine on her own. Still, she could hardly blame them for caring, so she steeled herself. "Yes, Simmons?"

"It's unacceptable!" the butler announced. "I've known Master Robert since he was in short coats and his lack of communication is deplorable. When I see him again, I shall be hard pressed not to let him know my feelings."

"That's quite kind of you, but unnecessary. I'm sure there's a reason for his silence. We'll know what it is when he gets here."

"I'm sorry, Miss Charlotte, but how long would it take the lad to dash off a letter? Why, I write more often to my mother, and she can't even read!" Simmons was now puffed up like an angry pheasant. "He's off kicking his heels while he still can, and has left you alone here. Meanwhile, your mother has left you in the care of a chaperone who is a complete scattergibbet!"

"Why, Simmons! I thought you liked my Aunt Verity."

He flushed, his stern expression softening. "I do. Lady Barton has always been kind, but she's been here for three days now and has done nothing but nap all day whist you ride off to God knows where!"

"I'm perfectly safe within the borders of Nimway."

"Balesboro Wood is not to be trifled with. It is haunted and filled with spirits. Why, Miss Caroline—" He stopped, folding his mouth into an unforgiving line.

"My sister was thrown from a horse and hit her head," Charlotte said, her voice ice cold. "It would not have mattered whether she was in Balesboro, or in the forecourt here at Nimway, the outcome could, and most likely would, have been the same."

Simmons flinched. "Miss Charlotte, please . . . I'm sorry. I just worry. We all do."

The butler's sincerity soothed Charlotte's ire, and after a brief struggle, she sighed. "Oh, stop looking as if I'm about to spit fire. I'll come to no harm in Balesboro, with or without a chaperone. It's a forest and is filled with trees and squirrels and birds and nothing more." *Except the occasional devastatingly handsome Italian man.*

It was a welcome relief to think about something other than Caroline's death or the servants' oppressive watchfulness. If Charlotte closed her eyes right now, she could remember every detail of that ardent kiss. It had been so heated, so passionate, so *perfect*, that she couldn't believe it had happened.

But it had. *And my, how I enjoyed it.* She supposed that was wrong of her; women weren't supposed to enjoy kisses, were they? If she followed the expectations of society, then she was to arrive at the altar untouched and unkissed, which seemed wrong in so many ways. How was she to know she'd found true love without such an experience? It was rather sad that Robert had never tried to kiss her, a fact which stung her pride now that she thought about it. Perhaps *that* was why she'd been so willing to kiss a stranger in the woods. Marco had made her feel wanted.

A weaker woman might have given in to temptation and placed herself back in his path. Although it had been a struggle, Charlotte had fought her baser instincts and had stayed away from the man for three whole days. That said quite a bit about her fortitude, for she'd thought about him a lot.

Too much, in fact.

Unaware of how far her thoughts had strayed from the topic of chaperones, Simmons added, "Your mother thought having a chaperone was important, or she wouldn't have invited Lady Barton here to begin with. I believe that if Mrs. Harrington had known that her ladyship would do nothing more than sleep all day, she wouldn't have left you in her care."

Charlotte took a sip of her tea. "You're right, Simmons."

Simmons looked relieved. "Thank you, miss."

"Aunt Verity does sleep a lot. I hope she's not taking ill."

The butler's face fell. "Lady Barton sleeps during the day because she is up all hours of the night reading risqué novels, most of them written in *French*." He said the word as if it were a viper and might bite him. "As much as I love and respect her lady-ship, I would *not* call her attentive. Why, you were out riding for four hours yesterday and in the rain, no less, and when Lady Barton came down to dinner, not only did she not realize you'd been gone all afternoon, but she was surprised to find out it had been raining, as well!"

"I came to no harm, so it makes no difference." Charlotte place her cup back into its saucer. "My aunt is doing an excellent job. She was kind to even come, for I'm sure she'd rather be enjoying the amusements of town than stuck here in the countryside."

Besides, to be honest, Charlotte had enjoyed the freedom of this last week. She'd loved riding Angelica through the fields in the rain, something she hadn't done since Caroline's accident as such things now sent Mama into instant hand-wringing angst.

Charlotte had missed her rainy-day rides, and this one had been every bit as delightful as she'd remembered – the rain fresh on her face, the cool air prickling her cheeks, the scent of crushed grass under her horse's hooves as Angelica pranced happily through fields and down muddy lanes, as ecstatic as Charlotte at their antics.

Charlotte smiled at the worried butler. "Simmons, please. I'm no longer a sickly child, a fact that you and the other servants would do well to remember."

"We know that, miss, but I fear that Miss Caroline's accident has put us all on watch. We don't wish the family to face more tragedy."

"Neither do I, which is why I promise to be cautious. As I've said, I'll be fine. Truly, I will."

Simmons looked as if he might say something more, but after a moment, he bowed. "Yes, miss. If you don't need anything more, then I'll see to it that Lady Barton's missives are placed on her breakfast tray."

"That would be lovely. Thank you." Charlotte waited for the butler to close the door behind him before she threw her napkin on the table, sprang to her feet, made her way to one of the windows. Outside, the sunshine beckoned, the breeze bobbing through the flowers as it swept to the lawn and then rippled across the lake.

She drew in a deep breath and rested her forehead against the cool glass.

Oh, how she hated being watched over! It brought back memories of the hours she'd spent as a child in treatments for her back, bound up in a horrible brace, or strapped to a contraption that tugged at her from all angles – So many efforts, and none had worked. She hated those hours and days with a passion so fierce that it sometimes frightened her, even now. Even more important, those experiences had made her yearn for the unfettered freedom of the outdoors. That was why she was so protective of her rides, and why she had to fight the urge to lash out when Simmons, or anyone else, suggested she shouldn't go, or that she should take someone with her. That was *her* time. Hers and no one else's.

Her breath had fogged the glass, and now she traced her finger through the misted pane to write 'Marco' in flourishing letters. Try as she might, she couldn't forget that kiss. Even now, if she closed her eyes, she could feel the warmth of his mouth over hers, the pressure of his hands as they molded her to him, the—

She shivered, suddenly more restless than ever, her face heated. She wiped his name from the window and then went to one of the new ornate mirrors that flanked the windows, grimacing at the sight of her red face. She placed her hands over her hot cheeks to cool them. *That darned kiss keeps leaving its mark.*

"Blast you, Marco di Rossi," she said under her breath. For some reason, she repeated his name, this time twirling the *r* into a purr. She had to laugh at own silliness. *I'm just giddy at the attention. No one has ever looked at me in such a way, especially not a man like that.*

He was intriguing. Too much so. Several times a day since that meeting, she'd had to fight a painfully strong impulse to visit him. But the more she'd wanted to go, the more she'd stayed away. The last thing she needed was a complication like that.

Sighing, Charlotte smoothed her hair, pausing to re-pin a stray lock. Finally satisfied she no longer looked flustered, she turned from the mirror. She'd go see Aunt Verity. A little company right now would not be amiss and would certainly keep her from thinking too much about things she shouldn't.

As she made her way to the stairs, she absently glanced into the open doors of the dining room, and slowly came to a halt.

Before she'd left, Mama had made certain the dining room was prepared for the coming renovations. The long mahogany table and chairs had been carried to the far side of the room, well away from the fireplace where they were protected by an off-white army of dust covers. Everything else – curtains, decorations, and paintings – had been carefully packed away and stored in empty guest rooms, where they'd remain until the work was completed.

Which was why the sight of a candleholder resting on the mantel over the fireplace had stopped Charlotte. Imagining the peel Mama would ring over the head of the thoughtless footman who'd forgotten his orders to leave the room untouched until the renovations were complete, Charlotte turned from the stairs and made her way to the dining room.

It was one of her favorite rooms. Long and elegant, the room was defined by tall windows and aged oak wainscoting. Like the great hall, hints of an older era lingered in the ornate woodwork that covered almost every surface. Overhead, large chandeliers hung, fastened in place by thick chains and requiring hundreds of candles for just one dinner.

The fireplace itself was built for massive four-foot logs, but the sheer size of it made the mantelpiece, a modest and overly simple affair, appear woefully out of place. *No wonder Mama wishes to change it. The proportion is all wrong.*

It was odd the things one accepted as 'right' when faced with them day in and day out. Shaking her head at her own blindness, Charlotte reached the fireplace only to realize the object sitting on the mantel wasn't a candleholder at all, but a golden scaled claw that reached up to clutch a moonstone the size of a fist. *What on earth is this?* She had no idea, but it was intriguing, and so heavy that she had to use both hands to pick it up. *It must be gold, to weigh so much.* She held it up to the light and then slid her thumb over the moonstone, surprised to find it warm.

She'd always loved moonstones, but Mama held them in aversion. This one was particularly pure of form, the glossy white surface reflecting the morning light. "Where did you come from?" she murmured.

As if in answer, the stone gleamed. Silver and white mists swirled just under the surface. And then there, in the stone's mists, a figure formed.

She caught her breath and looked closer. A man sat in a chair . . . and not just any man, but Marco di Rossi. He leaned forward, his elbows resting on his knees, his gaze piercing and direct. His finery was gone and in its place a pair of black breeches tucked into high riding boots, his broad chest and arms covered by a flowing white shirt that hung open at the neck. His hair was no longer in a neat que, but hung loose about his unshaven face, his expression every bit as dark as his eyes.

One look at those eyes and Charlotte was hit with a desire so instant and raw that her body ached with restless need. *Good God, what is this?* And yet try as she might, she couldn't seem to release the clawed metal or stop staring at the figure in the stone.

Defiant even in repose, he looked like what he was – dark, dangerous, and forbidden. *He belongs to another place, another home, and eventually, another woman.* The thought was as clear as the floor beneath her feet, and yet her fingers slid over the moonstone as if to touch him through the mist.

She grimaced at her actions. "Why are you doing this?" she muttered both to herself and the stone.

"It will not answer," came a deep, richly accented voice behind her.

She whirled, clutching the stone before her like a shield. There, sitting in a chair was Marco, looking just as she'd seen him. The flowing shirt parted at his tanned, powerful throat, his dark gaze locked on her. He was disheveled, his hair mussed as if he'd raked his hand through it over and over, his face shadowed with stubble.

She hadn't seen a vision in the stone at all, but a reflection. *How could I have thought otherwise*, she asked herself. "Mr. di Rossi, I didn't see you. What are you doing here?"

"Please. It's Marco, as I said before." He leaned back, draping an arm over the back of his chair, and she realized he was far more dangerous without his fine trimmings. "I should ask you that same question," he said, "but I saw what you were doing; you were talking to a rock."

Her face heated and she lowered the moonstone, although she found herself reluctant to release it. "I was talking to myself, not the rock. And you?"

"I was thinking," he said. He'd been doing more than that, for a sheaf of paper rested within reach on an empty chair, a stick of charcoal atop it, while crumpled pages lay scattered around his feet.

She nodded toward the papers. "It appears you've been sketching."

"That is how I think. I must decide what to carve for the fireplace pillars. I cannot begin until I have a general idea of how they will look, so I sketch."

His voice, rich and deep, stroked along her skin and she had to fight to keep her breath. "It's been three days and you don't have any idea what to carve? That's sadly inept, isn't it?"

The blazing look Marco sent her made her wince and she rushed to add. "I'm sorry. That's not what I meant to say. It's not inept; that's the wrong word. It's surprising, that's all. It seems you would just sketch something, and then begin." She tumbled over her words, saying them so fast even she couldn't hear them all. *Blast my unruly tongue! Just be quiet,* she told herself fiercely. It always happened like this; a situation would grow awkward and she'd blurt out the wrong thing in the wrong tone and make things worse.

"You cannot rush inspiration," he said shortly, sitting forward as if he were tempted to launch from his chair. "You do not snap your fingers and it comes running like a trained dog. You have to wait for it, coax it."

"I wasn't—" She bit her lip. "I shouldn't have spoken. I sometimes say things without thinking. I don't know why, but it just comes out and it always sounds far worse than I meant, and— Well, I'm sorry."

His gaze never wavered from her face, but some of the tension left him. After a long moment, he said thoughtfully, "It is not often I meet someone who will admit their flaws."

"Oh, I have plenty," she said with a rueful smile. "Shall I list them?"

His eyes warmed with humor. "Do we have the time? I've only three weeks to finish this project."

She laughed, and lowered the moonstone to her hip, resting it there. "I'll spare you, then."

He leaned back in the chair, the wood creaking as he did so.

She suddenly realized that he hadn't stood when she'd entered the room, which was basic courtesy. But she rather like his casualness, for it allowed her to be the same. "I hope you find your inspiration soon."

"I will. You mother was quite thorough. Before I came, she sent the measurements of the existing fireplace. I've already completed the mantelpiece, header, and trim panels. I carved them at my studio at home, and had them brought here. Now, all I have left are the pillars. I wanted to see the room before I made any decisions, as they require the most artistry."

She had no idea what any of those things were – a header, trim panels, pillars – but she knew what a mantel was, so she nodded as if she understood. "I hope you don't mind my asking, but how do you find your muse?"

"You don't. She must find you. All you can do is surround yourself with things that inspire her to speak."

Charlotte absently ran her thumb over the moonstone. For some reason the simple gesture soothed her jumpy heart. "I hope you find it soon, for this fireplace is sadly insufficient. Will the pieces you've already completed fit?"

"Easily, but now that I see the room and have studied the light, I realize the pillars must be larger than I'd originally thought."

The moonstone weighed heavily, so she shifted it forward so it would no longer dig into her hip.

Her movement caught Marco's gaze. "What is that?" he asked.

"I have no idea. I've never seen it before." She raised her brows. "It's not yours?"

"It was on the mantel when I came in. I'd never seen it before today." His eyes shimmered with humor. "You, meanwhile, were talking to that stone while staring into it as if finding life's secrets."

"It's pretty." She looked down at it now, noting that the moonstone still glowed softly. "It could be a paperweight."

"That base would not work. It would mark papers."

She curled her nose. Practical people were so annoying. "So it's not a paperweight. And I know it's not a candlestick, as there's no place to hold a candle. Maybe it's a—Ah! Perhaps it's a finial for a bed or something."

"A finial?"

"For the posts. Although it's so heavy, I can't see how it would remain fixed in place." She tilted her head to one side and squinted at it, hoping another view might help. "It could be an ornamental end for a staircase railing, but moonstones are notoriously delicate, so I doubt that. Maybe it's a—"

"For the love of God, woman." He arose with a lithe movement and strode across the rug to where she stood. He held out his hand. "Let me see that blasted thing."

It was an imperious gesture and she was tempted to refuse, but for some reason, his impatience amused her, so she handed him the stone.

He took it, hefting it one hand. "It could be a doorstop."

"Does it weigh enough?"

"No," he said reluctantly. "Not for the size of doors in this house."

She nodded. Like many very old houses, the huge oak doors had been designed to make enemies quake as they imagined giants walking the halls.

He flipped the object over and examined the base. "The carving is ornate." His brows knit, he peered closer. "It's old. Ancient even. As many carvings and sculptures as I've examined, I've never seen this particular style before." He brushed his thumb over the gold claw, rubbing it back and forth.

She tried not to look at his hands and failed, her mouth going dry. His hands were large and calloused, beautifully formed and yet strong. As an artist's hands should be, she decided. She hadn't paid Robert's hands much attention, but she was certain they didn't look like these.

Until now, she hadn't realized how disappointing that was.

Marco held the object up to the light and the moonstone

gleamed anew, casting a warm shadow over his stubbled face. "I wonder . . ." He held it out, as if to visualize it in use. "Ah! I know what it is. It's the head of a royal mace or scepter."

A royal mace. Fascinating. She looked at it with wonder. "It's beautifully made."

"It's well done." He shrugged. "But I've seen better."

As if it had been bumped by an invisible hand, the mace head flipped to one side, falling from Marco's grasp. He tried to catch it, but it slipped through his fingers and landed squarely on his foot.

She winced at the solid thud of metal hitting his leather boot. Marco cursed through clenched teeth, muttering a string of Italian invectives that made her glad she only knew the barest rudiments of the language.

He left the mace head on the floor and limped a few steps away, shaking his foot as if to shed the pain. Every step or two, he'd cast a furious glare at the stone, still muttering vivid curses.

Fearful for the safety of the unruly moonstone, Charlotte scooped it up and returned it to the mantel where she'd found it.

"That *thing* should be tossed into that lake you're so fond of riding around," he declared, his teeth still clenched.

She shot him a curious look. "How do you know I've been riding the lake path?"

"It doesn't matter," he snapped. "Just get rid of that cursed thing!"

"I like it. You should be more careful how you handle it. It's an antique, as you said, and moonstones are fragile."

"That 'fragile' moonstone broke my toe."

She cocked a disbelieving look at him. "You think it's broken?"

He moved his foot in a careful circle. "Perhaps not," he admitted reluctantly, though his scowl remained in place.

"Keep moving it," she ordered. "A few more minutes and your toe won't even hurt."

Reluctant amusement softened his ire. "You don't know that."

"No," she admitted. "But I'm hoping it's true."

"Hope has never cured a broken toe."

"As far as you know," she retorted. She glanced at the mace head where it sat on the mantel. "I wish I had three more to use as finials. I'd rather have them mounted on my bedposts than the carved pineapples Mama has put there." She made a face. "It's a wonder they haven't given me nightmares."

"You think four scaled claws holding oddly gleaming stones would give you fewer nightmares than some harmless pineapples?"

"At night, the pineapples look like angry faces. Compared to them, this is a beautiful piece of art."

"Yes, well, you didn't even know what that bloody thing was before I figured it out, so . . . ." He shrugged.

"I know now. It's a mace head," she said in a smug tone. "A *royal* mace head. I know because an art expert told me."

Marco's toe hurt too much for him to laugh, but he couldn't help a reluctant smile. She was as charming and fresh as the morning sun. She was quick witted, this intriguing woman, flashing between awkward pronouncements to good-humored teasing so quickly that it was dizzying. Her spirit was a heady mixture of cautious pride and mischievous innocence, and the combination was shockingly potent.

Even now, he found himself wondering what she'd do if he pulled her to him and kissed her smile from her soft lips, drinking from them like sweet wine.

"Admit it," she said. "The mace head is beautiful."

No, you are beautiful, not that ridiculous carving. "I am no expert on random metal and stone objects. All I know is this: I don't trust that blasted claw, and with reason." He eyed it now. Right before it fell on his foot, it had twisted from his grasp as if leaping on its own power. Almost as if it hadn't liked what he'd just said—

Good God, I'm conjecturing on what a vexatious hunk of metal thinks. What madness is this? What was it about this place, this woman, that made his mind leap to the most impossible thoughts?

Unaware he was now questioning his own sanity, she mused aloud, "I'll ask Simmons how it came to be here. He knows everything that happens under this roof, so—" Her own words seemed to catch her, for she stopped and looked at Marco. "Simmons knew you were here."

"Of course he does. Surely you didn't think I'd snuck in through a window like a thief?" He could see from the pink rising in her cheeks that she'd thought exactly that. "I've been visiting at different times of the day so I can observe how the light moves through the room. Your butler's only request was that I shouldn't wander into the rest of the house, which I was more than happy to promise."

"If you'd dressed the way I first saw you, I daresay he would have allowed you to go wherever you wished."

God, but he loved it when she let her gaze roam over him, as warm and intimate as a touch. He found it especially gratifying when he remembered that she'd ignored him for nigh on three entire days now.

His pride had been wounded by that. After their kiss in the woods, he'd wrongly believed she would use her assigned task of overseeing his progress on the fireplace as an excuse to visit him. Like a fool, he'd even attempted to keep his workshop clear of annoying dust in preparation of her visit. But she'd made no effort to see him.

To make matters worse, every morning since that day, he'd watched from his workshop window as she rode out into the misty morning forest on the back of her white mare.

He'd come to hate that blasted window. *Thank God I'm not home or my brothers and sisters would recognize my folly and tease me mercilessly.*

They would be right to do so, too. The sad fact was that he was spoiled. Women loved an artist. And as an artist, he had an endless appreciation of the beauty of the female face and body, of the hollows and shadows, of the soft lines and graceful curves. He loved their shy and seductive smiles, their soft laughter, and – when the mood suited him – their heated embraces in a rumpled bed. Women, young and old, vied for his attention and never had one ignored him.

All except this one, who chose instead to eye him with all the enthusiasm of a lamb facing a rabid wolf.

She tucked a fallen strand of hair behind her ear. "I should leave you to your work." She turned from the mantel and walked away, limping toward the door.

He'd noticed that limp when she'd come into the room, but had forgotten it while examining that cursed mace head. "Wait."

She turned to look at him.

"You're limping. Did you—"

"Don't."

The word cut him off as cleanly as a sharpened knife, her shoulders so stiff that he caught himself before he spoke again. "I'm sorry," he said cautiously. "Have I said something wrong?"

She took several steps away, and he could tell she was now painfully aware of her uneven gait, as it worsened with each step. Face red, she stopped by the line of chairs near the wall which he'd just left, her hands trembling where she smoothed her skirts. "I limp," she said shortly. "It is not an injury."

"You don't need to say more."

"I won't."

He thought back to when they'd met in the woods. She'd walked with an uneven gait then, he realized with some surprise, but he'd blamed it on the rough forest floor. Aware she still watched him, he shrugged. "Whatever it is, I don't give a damn. Not one."

Her gaze had grown shadowed and she watched him with her lashes lowered.

Was she wondering how much she should tell him? How much

he deserved to know? Very little, he decided regretfully. "I'm sorry if I made you uncomfortable," he said quietly. "I was just concerned."

Her expression darkened instantly. "I don't need more people worrying about me!"

"Then I won't."

Her gaze narrowed.

"I mean it." He spread his hands wide. "If you say you don't need me to worry about you, then I'll stop."

She looked at him a minute, an array of emotions flickering over her expressive face. Finally, her shoulders slumped, and she grimaced. "I'm being ridiculous. I'm just tired of people acting as if I'm unable to care for myself."

"I never—"

"My spine is crooked." The words ripped from her lips with the rat-a-tat-tat of a hard rain. "I was not born this way, but as I grew, my back began to curve. My parents brought doctors and physicians and even charlatans to Nimway." A haunted look entered her eyes. "But nothing helped."

"The treatments were difficult." He didn't ask, for her expression said it all.

She nodded. "They tried potions, oils, braces, and – Oh God, everything. It got a little worse each year until I stopped growing. That put an end to it. It has gotten no worse for years now, and the doctors have left. So I am what I am and I can live with that."

She lived with it very well, he decided. "You didn't need to tell me all of this, but I appreciate your trust."

She rubbed her forehead. "I'm not sure why I told you. But perhaps it's better that I did. People notice, of course. Most of the time they won't ask, which I prefer. Some of them stare when they think I'm not looking, which I hate, while others avoid looking at me at all, as if I were invisible."

"I can see you perfectly well, even when you're telling me my toe is not broken, when I know it is."

She chuckled, humor washing away her irritation. "Thank you."

"For what?"

"For not repeating empty platitudes or pitying me. I can't stand either."

"I could never pity you; I've seen you ride that brute of a mare you call a horse."

A hint of satisfaction warmed her smile. "Angelica can be a handful."

"Not for you. I've watched you ride out each and every morning since I arrived, and you never falter." He leaned forward. "I know your secret."

Her expression shuttered, though her smile remained in place. "Secret?"

"Oh yes. You might sedately trot that beast from the stables with you looking like a maiden of meek and proper manners, but as soon as you're out of view of prying eyes, you set that animal to a wild gallop and ride until it must feel as if you're flying."

Her eyes sparkled. "It does. I don't limp when I ride."

"No one does. If we're to be honest, I must admit that I hadn't noticed this curve you've mentioned. But then I've been too busy admiring other parts of you. Your eyes, your hair, the boldness of your nose—"

She slapped her hand over her nose.

He chuckled. "Don't cover it. I find your nose is fascinating or I wouldn't have mentioned it. There are more parts of you that I admire, but sadly, as they were involved in a kiss that never happened, I can say no more."

This time she was the one who laughed. God, but it was good to see the sadness disappear from her eyes. He felt as if he'd accomplished something worthwhile. Something exquisite.

Still chuckling, her gaze dropped to the discarded papers he'd left crumpled on the floor which were now at her feet. Curiosity flickered over her face and she bent to pick one up, but he was quicker, scooping up the crumpled pages and carrying them to the fire. Soon they were sputtering in the flames.

"Why did you do that?"

"If they were good ideas, they wouldn't have been wadded up on the floor."

She watched the pages turn to ash. "There were a lot of them. That doesn't reflect well on your muse."

"My muse is a vengeful wench who finds it amusing to mislead me repeatedly." Satisfied his ruined sketches were where they belonged, he crossed his arms and watched them waft up the chimney, nothing left but glowing ashes.

She slanted him a look. "You have no idea what you're going to do with these pillars."

"Not yet, but I will."

"I'm surprised Mama gave you so much leeway."

Arms still crossed, he sighed and addressed the ceiling. "Do you hear the way this one insults me? She doubts me openly and will not even pretend she thinks me capable."

"Are you talking to your muse?"

"No, to God. No one else would believe what nonsense I must put up with for my art."

Her eyes twinkled with suppressed laughter. "I didn't mean to suggest you were incapable in any way, especially not the son of a famous painter." She shot him a curious glance. "Is that how my mother found you? Through your father?"

"No. I installed a number of statues in the garden of a convent in France, along with a large fountain. Your mother and father visited a few years later and admired my work. The abbess gave my name to your mother. Eight months ago, she wrote asking if I'd accept this commission."

"So you've never met?"

"Sadly, no. But if she likes my work, she's promised to recommend me to the Queen. That is why I accepted the offer, although it was generous enough on its own. Such a recommendation will lift my reputation. And if I can fulfill a commission for the Queen, then I am made."

"You are ambitious."

"I am," he admitted without hesitation. "I have a family that depends on me."

"Oh yes. All those brothers and sisters." Her smile slipped, and her gaze dropped to the fireplace. A log shifted, the noise echoing in the silence as a large ember landed on the hearth.

She moved away, keeping her skirts a safe distance from the flames.

He watched, admiring her slender, graceful hands where they held the blue silk of her gown. Something about her pulled at him, something beyond a heated kiss shared in a mystical wood. The way she moved and spoke, both impulsive and quick, contradicted the caution he saw in her blue gaze.

There were many layers to her, and to his chagrin, he wanted to know them all. "You must come to my workshop so that I may show you the pieces I've already finished." The words slipped from him as if pulled by a golden thread.

Good God, why had he said that? He hated letting people view his work until it was in place.

"I mustn't slow you down. The fireplace must be installed by —" Her lips closed over the words as if they refused to be spoken aloud. After a strained moment, she said, "Soon. We've an event, a formal breakfast. Hundreds of people have been invited." With a sudden burst of restlessness, she turned away, her skirts rustling with each step. "I must go."

"Charlotte?"

She pulled up short, but didn't turn to look at him.

He took a step toward her. "This breakfast? Why is it so important?"

She smoothed nervous hands over her skirt. "There's to be a wedding."

The words echoed in the large, nearly empty room. "Whose

wedding?" he asked harshly, although he already knew the answer.

"Mine." Her answer was almost a whisper. Head bowed, she left, her skirts rustling as she closed the door behind her with cold finality.

He stared at the door, oddly bereft at her answer. *What is wrong with me that I feel this so strongly?* But perhaps it wasn't that difficult to understand. He recognized her pride, admired her honesty, and reveled in her untamed nature. And what's more, he'd seen the flash of despair that darkened her eyes at unexpected moments. Was she being forced into this marriage? He couldn't imagine that to be true, for she was as strong willed as she was spirited. Yet he couldn't ignore the shadows that clung to her like tangled silk scarves.

Sighing, he picked up his charcoal and paper, and resumed his seat. He stared at the fireplace for a long time, the forgotten moonstone alone on the mantel.

After a while, he forced his mind to empty, closed his eyes, rested the charcoal on the paper, and drew. At first, his hand moved slowly, but as the image bloomed to life, his motions quickened. Soon, the charcoal raced across the page, each stroke sure and strong.

Finally, his hand stilled, and he opened his eyes.

The paper didn't contain a magnificent design for the pillars. Instead, a young woman stared out at him, her lips soft, her nose bold, her eyes the saddest he'd ever seen.

CHAPTER 5

Pietro squinted against the bright afternoon sun. "You are not working."

"I've worked morning and night for the last three days. Now, I am resting." Marco leaned against the doorframe of the wide door and crossed his arms, the fresh breeze tugging at his shirt. "Besides, the dust was making me cough."

"It's good you are making dust." Pietro nodded wisely. "The stone is talking to you."

"Finally," Marco agreed. "I will carve two women, Greek goddesses, one on each pillar. The mantel will rest above them."

The servant nodded thoughtfully, as if picturing it. "And?"

"That is all I have now, but the details are forming."

Pietro grunted his satisfaction. "It will come. You are well on your way to getting Mrs. Harrington's recommendation to the Queen, and we are that much closer to going home." He leaned against the opposite doorpost and, hands deep in his pocket, he looked out across the stable yard with an air of contentment.

It had been three days since Marco had last spoken to Charlotte. The day after their conversation, he'd returned to Nimway with the hope of speaking with her again, but Simmons's cold, suspicious stare had let Marco know that any attempt to find Charlotte alone would fail. Angry at himself for even trying, and feeling like a fool, he'd returned to his workshop and had thrown himself into his work. And here he'd stayed since. For the last three days, left alone with his thoughts, he'd relived every moment of their conversation, ending each time with her tortured whisper as she'd left the room. He was burning to discover why she found her coming marriage so distasteful. Was that what had caused the sadness that flickered through her eyes every so often, as raw and real as the ground beneath her feet?

A fresh, cool breeze blew through the wide open stable doors, tugging at Marco's shirt. Bees buzzed in the nearby flowers, while butterflies flitted in and out of the field where Diavolo and Goliath grazed. The scent of lavender and rose wafted from the gardens behind the house, mingling with the smell of fresh hay and oats.

Past the gardens, Nimway Hall warmed in the sun, sheltered by the ivy that climbed up its stone walls. The graceful sweep of the emerald colored lawn was threaded with white gravel pathways that led to the deep blue lake. Behind the lake, purple and yellow flowers nodded in the gentle breeze.

"The English know how to garden," Pietro said grudgingly "But they cannot grow grapes, sorry bastards."

Marco's gaze moved beyond the lake where a large, golden field stretched to Balesboro Wood. "It is beautiful here."

Pietro harrumphed. "Not as beautiful as Italy."

Marco gave the elderly, cantankerous stonemason an amused look. "You can love more than one place. It will not hurt you."

"Italy is home. Besides, Cook says it is very wet and gray here in the winter."

Marco cocked a brow at his servant. "You've been spending an inordinate amount of time in Nimway's kitchen of late. Is it because of this woman?"

"Someone told her that Italians are good lovers." Pietro looked smug. "So far, I have not abused her of that notion."

"It's good that we leave soon, before she discovers the truth. She might—" A white horse appeared from the depths of the wood. Marco watched as Charlotte guided the huge animal across the rough ground and onto the path around the lake. Today she wore a riding habit of hunter green, a white spill of lace at her neck, her dark red hair pinned beneath a tall riding hat that sported a pale green band with fluttering ends. Her long skirts flowed across the horse's white flanks, rippling with the breeze.

Marco straightened when Charlotte turned her horse toward the stables instead of onto the path that curved around the Hall. She usually rode Angelica to Nimway's front door where a groom waited to lead the animal back to the stables. But in the brief time Marco had been here, he'd noticed that on occasion, Charlotte would instead ride her horse to the stables where she'd busy herself chatting with the grooms and brushing the monster beast while ordering the stable hands to feed the animal a ridiculous number of apples.

Not that Marco had watched, of course. He was far too busy for such nonsense. But nothing kept her voice and her low, musical laughter from drifting into his workshop, which had been damned distracting.

Pietro cursed. "Stop that."

"Stop what?"

"Stop looking at her like that. As if you see a lovely puzzle only you can solve."

"You think I cannot solve this puzzle?"

"I don't want you to try," Pietro almost growled. "That woman is not for you."

The words hit Marco like icy water. "The only reason I'm interested in her is because she's been tasked with overseeing my work here." Which was a lie, and Marco knew it.

"Good. You know what would happen to your prospects if you

seduced the daughter of a noble patron. Not only would the recommendation to royalty disappear, but you would be disgraced, and then where would your family be?"

"It will not happen," Marco said sharply. "I'm not a fool; I will not sabotage my own success." Which didn't mean he wasn't tempted. God knew he was only human and the lush and lovely Charlotte presented a wealth of challenges. But it didn't take a genius to see the end result of this particular flirtation, no matter how pleasurable. "You need have no worries, she is engaged to wed," he said sourly. *Damn the man to hell and back again, whoever he is.*

"*Propio bourno!* This, I did not know." The servant gave a satisfied smile, revealing a row of wine-stained teeth. "When is the blessed event to occur?"

"In three weeks' time." Marco watched as Charlotte neared the fence that lined the far end of the stable yard.

The sun warmed her auburn hair, bringing out the gold tones. He noticed that as she led the horse, the animal's gait had changed slightly, as if she were matching Charlotte's limp. For a moment, it looked as if the two were dancing, horse and rider.

A stable hand hurried to open the gate, and Charlotte led her horse into the stable yard. There, she handed her horse to a waiting groom, her gaze swinging to meet Marco's.

For a long moment their gazes locked. Marco's chest tightened, and he wondered if he should cross the yard and speak to her. *To what end? There's nothing I could or should say. I've no reason to speak to her at all.*

Angelica butted her head against Charlotte's arm, drawing her rider's attention, and that was that – Charlotte turned away to take care of the demanding animal.

Marco muttered under his breath about evil creatures.

"You're still staring," Pietro pointed out.

"Go to hell," Marco snapped and then wheeled about and went back inside, welcoming the safety of the cool, dark stable.

Pietro followed. "I don't understand. She's not your usual type of woman."

"And what is my 'usual' type?" Marco asked coldly.

"Tall, stately, and beautiful. This one is pretty, yes, but no more." The stonemason pursed his lips. "It's a pity about that limp, too. When she walks, you can see that one hip is higher than the other and—"

"She is fine as she is," Marco said coldly, his jaw aching where he clenched it. "We are all different, Pietro. It is those differences which reveal beauty. If we all looked the same—" He shrugged. "Everything would be bland, uninteresting, boring, and ugly."

"I suppose so." The stonemason frowned. "I hadn't thought of it like that."

"You should think more. It will do you good. Besides, I am not so arrogant as to change what God has deemed perfect. You should do the same."

The old stonemason cast a pious look heavenward and crossed himself. "I cannot argue with that. But I will say one thing, and you will not like it."

"Then do not say it."

"You need to hear it." The old man pointed a gnarled finger. "You are making an error. Ever since we arrived, you've been distracted, moping around the shop, unable to hear the stone when it speaks to you. You cannot work well because you are constantly looking for that woman, wondering about her. You watch her as if you would devour her."

"You are exaggerating."

"Ha! You know what I think? *E' stato un colpo di fulmine.*"

"Like hell," Marco snapped. He didn't believe in *colpo di fulmine.* Ancient Italian lore held that a passionate man could, with just one glance at the right woman, be hit with a consuming ardor so strong that it would be as if he'd been struck by lightning and his chest split open, his love exposed for all the world to see. The English called it 'love at first sight,' which was a pale version of the same foolish myth. "Spare me your ridiculous talk. I feel nothing more than admiration for Charlotte Harrington."

His admiration was well deserved, too. His artist's instincts were intrigued by her fiery color, the delicate yet stubborn line of her jaw, by the boldness of her nose, by the fullness of her lips. But more than her physical attractions, Marco was fascinated by her many expressions and her bravery in facing the challenges of her life. And there were so many things he didn't yet know about her. Why did she ride into the woods each day as if pursued by the hounds of hell? Why had she looked so unsettled when she mentioned her coming marriage? But most of all, why was there such sadness behind her amazing blue eyes?

The old man sighed loudly, drawing Marco's attention once again. "I don't mean to argue—"

"Really?"

"But don't forget why we're here. What you stand to lose if you stray from the rules of a commission."

"The rules of a commission," Marco repeated in a bitter tone. "That the satisfaction of the patron is more important than the quality of the art? That the artist is never to assume he is more than a common laborer and never cross the social boundaries established to keep it so?"

"It is the way things are," Pietro said stubbornly. "You know that."

Marco looked down at his hands, which were clenched into fists. With a deep, heartfelt sigh, he stretched out his fingers, noting the callouses from holding the chisels and hammer, the dust that had been ground into his fingertips that no amount of soap could wash away, the cuts and bruises caused by working with stone that was sharp and unwieldy. They weren't the hands of a person born into the gentry, someone who could court and win a woman like Charlotte Harrington.

He curled his hands back into fists. "I've work to do," he growled. "Sharpen my chisel. I will need it this afternoon." Jaw set,

Marco tossed aside the dust cover that hid the pillars from sight and examined the work he'd done so far. A figure was beginning to emerge from each pillar, although the specific shape wasn't yet discernable. But inspiration was coming and even now, the excitement of it flickered through him, his fingers itching to pick up a hammer and chisel and set to work.

Behind him, Pietro shifted items on one of the long work tables. He found the sharpener and set to work, and the calming sound of the chisel sliding across the whet stone soon rang out.

Gratified to see some progress on the pillars, Marco threw the dust cover over them, and then cast a satisfied look around the workshop. They were housed in an older portion of the stable complex which branched off the newer building. Together, they formed an L shape. The space was crude, but effective. The ceiling was high, and there was a surfeit of natural light from the many windows. A woodstove had been installed at one end and provided welcome warmth during the chilly spring nights.

The ground was of hard-packed dirt, which suited his purpose well as the dust clung to it instead of drifting through the air. Several stalls, which he suspected had been used as tack rooms prior to his arrival, had been emptied for his use. Someone had furnished the farthest room with a cot, a small stove, and a surprisingly comfortable chair. It was warm and private, and far from Pietro who snored as if he were the lone angel singing in a heavenly choir.

"There." The stonemason placed a newly sharpened chisel into an open leather case. "I can sharpen the others if they need—" His gaze locked on something just past Marco. The old man's brows knit over his large nose. "What is that?"

Marco turned. There, sitting in the middle of his work table on a stack of discarded drawings, was the royal mace head, the moonstone catching the early afternoon light where it beamed in one of the windows. "Where in the hell did that come from?"

"It wasn't there a few minutes ago." Pietro rubbed his whiskered chin. "At least, I don't *think* it was there. What is it?"

"It's the head of a royal mace."

"Like a king might use?"

Or a queen. "Yes." Marco went to the mace head, his gaze falling on the creased pages that rested under the metal base. The edges of the pages were charred. From the top sheet, a familiar face stared back at him.

Cursing, he moved the mace head aside and picked up the papers. "How did these get here?"

"They look burned."

"They should be ashes," Marco said grimly as he flipped through the pages. Charlotte's familiar face peered back at him in sketch after sketch. In some of them she smiled; in some, a hot, impatient look flashed from her fine eyes; in others her mouth was thinned, her chin angled with haughty pride.

He scowled at his own foolishness. Over the last few days, in an attempt to beguile his muse into revealing the figures in the pillars, he'd free sketched various ideas. Normally, sketching was a tried and true way to stir his imagination. But to his chagrin, ever since their conversation in the dining room, he'd caught himself sketching Charlotte instead the pillars. Over and over and over.

Marco refolded the sketches and turned to his servant. "Did you pull these from the stove?"

"Of course not!" Pietro huffed as he eyed the stack of sketches. "What are they?"

"Nothing of importance," Marco muttered. He folded the stack in half and carried it back to the stove, and tossed the sketches into the flames. This time, he watched them burn. As the last paper curled into ashes, he closed the stove door. "I tossed them into the fire last night, but someone retrieved them before they were destroyed."

"It wasn't me." The stonemason's wrinkled face creased into a frown. "Do you think one of the grooms might have been here? We haven't been locking the doors."

"Why would they pull sketches from the fire?"

"Perhaps Miss Harrington asked them to do it. You're not one to share your ideas. Maybe she wanted more information about the carvings than you've given her."

"That is ludicrous," Marco scoffed. "She wouldn't—" He frowned.

"What is it?"

"The last time I spoke to her was in the dining room. She started to pick up some drawings I'd tossed to the floor. I took them from her and threw them in the fire, much as I did these."

"Well, then. There you have it." Pietro seemed to think that solved everything. "She is determined to find out what your designs are for the fireplace."

"If she wanted to see my work, she has only to walk through that door, and I'd show it to her. She knows that." He returned to his work table where the mace head sat waiting. Sunshine poured through the window and warmed the metal claw to a rich gold, which made Marco think of the golden threads that shimmered in Charlotte's auburn hair when she stood in the sunshine. She might be avoiding him as if he were the plague, but when she'd looked at him across the stable yard, he'd felt as if she'd been hoping he'd do something more than stare back. *What do you want from me? That I should speak to you? Reach out in some way? But to what end?*

He'd already invited her to visit him. Plus, she already had the perfect excuse to visit his workshop – her own mother had seen to that. No, Charlotte hadn't yet visited him for one reason – she knew as well as he did that every time they came together, sparks flew. *I am not the only one who feels it, am I, carissima?*

"You're smiling."

Marco banished his smile. "Was I? I was considering what you said. I don't think Charlotte had anything to do with my sketches being rescued from the fire. Not this time, anyway."

"Charlotte?" Pietro's thick brows knitted over his nose.

Marco could have bitten his own tongue. "I meant Miss Harrington, of course," he amended himself coolly.

The old man muttered a string of curses. "You must finish this project as soon as possible. Just carve some cherubs holding a—a—a garland of flowers, or a vase, or some such nonsense, and be done with it."

"This commission is too important, and my work must be perfect."

Pietro looked as if he had a million other things to say, none of them good, but after a moment, he said glumly, "You're right. It must be perfect."

"And it will be. Now go. Return to the kitchens and find us some lunch. And stop worrying about Miss Harrington. Instead, you should worry about yourself. You're the one flirting with a powerful woman. If you anger Cook, then for the rest of our stay we will be eating burned, moldy toast and undercooked gristle."

"I will keep her happy." Pietro hesitated. "Are you sure you don't need me here?"

"What for? I cannot carve while you're holding my hand."

Pietro flushed and muttered something about artists being too touchy for their own good. "Fine. I'll fetch lunch." He headed for the door, smoothing back his hair as he went.

Marco watched the old stonemason make his way down the path toward the Hall, his step growing livelier as he neared the kitchens.

Smiling to himself, Marco returned to his work table. He pushed the moonstone out of the way, opened his folio, and removed the drawings he'd made of the pillars.

His gaze flickered back to the fire and his thoughts returned to the sketches he'd burned. It was a pity he hadn't kept at least one of them so that when he returned to Italy, he'd have something to remember Charlotte by—

Thunk! The moonstone fell, tipping over a small pot. Black ink splashed onto the table, soaking into the thirsty foolscap, and pooling around a line of charcoal pencils. Marco grabbed his folio just before the river of ink reached it, and stuck it high on a shelf.

Damn it all, he didn't need this mess! Cursing to the high heavens, he picked up the soaked papers and carefully carried them to the stove where he tossed them inside, slamming the door for good measure. He pulled a rag from a stack kept nearby and, muttering about cursed moonstones, he washed his hands in a water bucket by the door.

Most of the ink came off, and he took grudging solace in the fact that the rest would disappear in a day or so. But the accident was a sign. Pietro was right; the time had come to focus on the real task at hand.

Marco returned to his work table and cleaned it as well as he could. That done, he moved the moonstone to a less polluted corner of the table. "Not that you deserve to be rescued from a mess of your own making," he told the cursed carving. "But God knows what ink might do to a moonstone—"

Charlotte's voice lifted through the open windows.

He leaned forward to catch her words. She was telling a groom that Angelica needed to be brushed, and something else he couldn't quite hear. He held his breath, waiting, and then caught sight of his reflection in the moonstone.

His expression was intense, hopeful, hungry. *Damn it all. What am I doing?* "Enough!" he announced angrily, shoving the mace head far away. He found a clean piece foolscap and a new stick of charcoal. It took all of his self-discipline, but with more determination than vision, he forced himself to focus on his work. "I must finish this," he told himself grimly. "Or else."

"Or else what?"

He turned.

Charlotte stood in the doorway, the sun warm on her shoulders and lighting a nimbus of gold around her auburn hair. "Good afternoon." She stepped into the darkness of his workshop and looked about her with an air of curiosity. "I hope I'm not interrupting."

CHAPTER 6

"What are you doing here?" Marco winced at the harshness of his own voice. He couldn't help it; her mere presence crackled along his words like lightning over water.

Charlotte's expression, which had been open and even amused, instantly changed. It was as if a shutter had been drawn, for her smile disappeared, and her lashes lowered, hiding her expression. She said in a cool tone, "You invited me, remember?"

He had. But he was finding that hoping to see her, and actually seeing her were two different things. Hoping to see her was like knowing someone would be serving his favorite berry torte after dinner. But seeing her in person was having the flavors of that berry torte melting in his mouth, the buttery crust lingering on his tongue, and the sweet scent of warm berries making him yearn for more.

He tried to ignore his overwrought senses. "I'm sorry if I sounded unwelcoming. I was just dealing with an irritating ink spill."

"Ah. That would irritate me, too." As she walked farther into the room, she took off her hat and tucked it under one arm. The hem of her habit and her fine leather boots were mud splattered, while her cheeks bloomed. "I came to see the portions of the fire-place that you've already finished."

"Of course." Some of her silky auburn hair had come loose from its pins, and long tendrils fell over her shoulder and clung to the lace at her neck. He wondered if could replicate the curl of her hair into one of the figures he was carving.

"I hope the ink spill didn't harm your sketches."

"Actually, it was more of an ink dousing."

"Was anything ruined?"

"Nothing of consequence," he lied.

"Good." Her gaze slid past him to the dark corners of his workshop and then back. "Where is your servant?"

"Pietro went to the kitchen. He is supposed to be fetching our lunch, although I think he's more interested in seducing your cook."

She smiled. "I must meet this servant of yours. He sounds like quite a character."

"He is more of one than he should be." Marco slipped the remaining sketches into the folio so that they were out of sight. "So . . . you've come to see what I've accomplished so far. I'm happy to show you what's already done."

"Mama will be glad for news of your progr—" Charlotte came to an abrupt halt, surprise flickering over her face. "How did *that* get here?"

Marco followed her gaze to the moonstone. "Ah yes. That." He looked back at her. "I was hoping you might have the answer to that."

"I didn't bring it here, if that's what you mean. I haven't seen it since I left it on the mantel in the dining room when we last spoke. I assumed Simmons had put it away somewhere."

"Apparently, he put it away here, on my work table. But please, when you leave, take that thing with you. It's been misbe-having and has knocked over an entire pot of ink onto my table."

"So that's what caused your ink dousing." Amusement warmed her eyes. "I hope you remembered to protect your toes."

"I did. Still, that cursed claw ruined some old sketches and left ink stains on my hands. As you can see, I have evidence of its perfidy." He held up his hands.

"Oh no!" She placed her hat on the table, and then crossed to him and took one of his hands between hers, her skin as soft as her touch was gentle. She examined his ink-stained hand, rubbing her fingers over one stain as if hoping to banish it then and there. "Those won't come off any time soon."

He looked down at her bent head and wondered why his heart thundered in such a way. He had to fight the urge to bend down and brush his lips against hers. He suddenly realized he was staring and struggled to remember what she'd just said. "I—That's quite all right. There is nothing on my social calendar this week."

She sent him a surprised look, although she kept his hand between her own, her skin warm on his. "Social calendar?"

He curled his fingers over hers, moving closer. He was pleased that although she flushed, she didn't move away. "It might surprise you to know that I waltz quite well. I also know how to bow properly and how to discern which forks and spoons should be used with which course. Artists are often thrown into society, much as ponies are invited to perform in the park."

Her lips curved into a smile. "You, sir, are no pony."

He lifted her hand and brush a kiss over her fingers. "No, I'm not."

Her face was so pink he was surprised it didn't catch afire. "Of course you know how to dance and how to properly wield your cutlery," she said. "I saw your fine clothing when you arrived. Besides, despite your lack of a fine coat today, your boots are not those of a common laborer."

"Ah, my boots. My biggest weakness. I have far more pairs than I should."

"So do I," she confessed. She traced her finger over the largest scar on his hand. The scar lined the edge of his thumb from his wrist to the nail. "Where did this come from?"

"The slip of a very sharp chisel. As you can see, my chosen career is not gentle."

She shook her head. "So many callouses and scars."

"Stone can be unforgiving." He thought she might release his hand then, but instead, she held it tighter and glanced up at him, a question in her eyes.

He was astounded once again at the color of her eyes. He'd seen many people with blue eyes, but none as dark as hers. In a certain light, they seemed almost purple.

"I wonder . . ." she began.

He waited. His hands felt as if they were afire, her touch both temptation and torture. He tried not to breathe too deeply of her scent, that of sunshine and lily, which went straight to his head like the richest red wines of his home. He cleared his throat. "What do you wonder?"

"My Aunt Verity's maid knows many ways to get stains out of garments. She might know of a solution that would help your poor hands. I'll ask her."

"Thank you." But he didn't want help, especially not with inconsequential ink stains. What he wanted was this woman in his arms, her lips under his, her heart beating against his own – *All of which you cannot have.*

Damn reality. Dispirited, he tugged his hand free, picked up a rag, and rubbed at the stains again. He knew it wouldn't help, but the movement gave him the space he needed to clear his head.

Disappointment flashed in her eyes, but she said nothing. She wandered a few steps away, picking up a chisel from his work table and pretending to examine it. After a moment, she dropped it back on the table. "You confuse me."

He threw down the rag. "How so?"

"You are an artist, but you have the air of someone born of the nobility. I know your father is a famous painter, but was he born of a famous house?"

"No, but my mother's family is one of the oldest and wealthiest in Italy. She died when I was young, so I don't remember much about her, and even less of her family."

"Her family? Not yours?"

"They disinherited her when she married my father. They thought him a lowly artist when he was, in fact, incredibly talent-ed." Marco leaned against the work table and crossed his arms over his chest. "My grandfather was a vindictive man and did what he could to destroy my father. The old man spread vile rumors and kept others from purchasing my father's work. It slowed my father's rise to fame by decades and made life for our family very difficult. But still, my mother was alive then, so my father was a happy man. He says those early years were like heaven, that the sun shone every day and the birds sang only the sweetest of songs."

"Your parents must have been happy to have had so many children."

"In Italy, large families are a way of life. My mother died shortly after giving birth to my youngest sister. My father was devastated, although he continued to paint. Portraits were his specialty, especially of the wealthy, and that meant he had to travel to his subjects. As an only parent, he found it difficult to be gone."

"He never remarried?"

"He's never shown the least interest. Eventually, he moved from portraits to painting landscapes, hoping to grow his market in a direction that would allow him to stay home. He thought he'd found the perfect situation when an art dealer from Milan offered to travel throughout the continent and sell his paintings for a simple commission."

"A perfect solution."

"At first, yes. My father had no head for business and he

thought the dealer would negotiate higher prices, even with the commission, but the man was a thief and he stole most of the profits. We did not find out until it was too late."

"Oh no! How old were you when this happened?"

"Too young to be of help. We faced some difficult years where just putting food on the table was a hardship."

"Why didn't your father just paint more pictures and then sell them himself?"

"Because shortly after he discovered the perfidy of the dealer, my father grew ill. I believe it was because of his anguish over what he'd lost. He's never truly recovered, and now his hands shake too much for him to control a brush."

"I hope that scoundrel was brought to justice," she said fervently.

"He was, but the paintings and money were gone, so—" Marco shrugged. "We were left without."

"What a betrayal." She started to say something, and then stopped. After a moment, she said in a hurt tone, "Life can be cruel."

"At times. Life isn't all happy or all sad. Instead, it's a fascinating mixture of both."

"Fascinating? How can you say that?"

"Because without the one, we would never appreciate the other."

She was silent a moment, her gaze dropping where the toes of her boots peeked from the skirts of her riding habit. "What does your father do now?"

"He helps with my career and keeps me from making the same mistakes he's made. Thanks to him, I am now the main caretaker of my family, although we all work. Two of my brothers are horse breeders, one has just harvested the first crop from his new vineyard, while the youngest is studying to be a physician."

"What of your sisters?"

"One dedicated herself to the church, and the other married an established farmer who owns acres of olive trees. They are blissfully happy, both of them." He shrugged. "So you see? Except for my father's health, life holds no ugliness for us now."

"It's nice your father can assist you."

"He's a better manager for me than he ever was for himself. He helps me decide which commissions will increase the value of my work and further my career. One of the things he's insisted upon is that, when in society, I should always dress as what I am, a born member of nobility."

"You are one, despite the meanness of your mother's family."

He grinned. "Only the Scots equal the Italians in their love of a good, centuries-long family feud. In fact, my father used his father-in-law's hard heart to my advantage. My grandfather was unkind to almost everyone he met so there were a great many noble families in Italy eager to – How do you English say it? Ah yes. Eager to put my grandfather's nose out of joint. Those were some of my first commissions, and they paid very, very well."

"That was very wise of your father."

"It was. Still, as he's pointed out time and again, as welcomed as those families have made me, inviting me to their supper tables and soirees, an artist must follow the rules of comportment and never put himself on a level with his betters. There will be no forgiveness if I cross that line."

"That seems unduly harsh."

He shrugged. "It is life. But he's seen it happen to others. My experiences and those of my father have taught me well. So long as I can answer the call of my passion, I will be content."

She frowned, her delicate eyebrows lowered. "Your passion. That is what sculpting is for you."

"It isn't just what I do, it's who I am."

She nodded, her brow still furrowed. "I haven't found my passion yet."

"You will."

"I hope so," she said wistfully.

He watched her as she walked to the window and looked out, her gaze distant and unseeing. *What is she thinking?* He was struck anew with the desire to kiss her. God, but never in his life had he been so beset with a mixture of curiosity and longing. What was happening to him?

He was a fool to even think of this woman in any way other than as what she was, the untouchable daughter of a sponsor. He'd never met Mrs. Harrington, but from the correspondence they'd shared, he knew the high level of pride she took in her family ancestral home. If he crossed the line of propriety with Charlotte, he was risking far more than he was willing to. He wasn't the sort of uncaring cad who throw his career and the future of his own family into the dirt for nothing more than the touch of a woman he had no business speaking to, much less longing after. *She is not for me. She will never be for me.*

She turned to say something, but stopped, her gaze moving over his face. His expression must have darkened with his thoughts, for she asked in a quiet, serious tone, "What is it?"

He shook his head, unwilling to put into words the thoughts that left his mouth tasting of ash.

As if his silence hurt her, she winced. After a long moment, she said, "We all have secrets, don't we?"

The hurt in her voice chipped at his heart. He wanted to reach for her, to sweep her against him and vow to never have a secret from her of any kind, but he remained where he was, glued in place, his heart so heavy it felt as if it were made of lead. It wasn't that he loved this woman, that was impossible for they'd only just met. It was that the air between them was filled with golden, exciting promise, and turning his back on that was the hardest thing he'd ever done. Though it cost him dearly, he nodded. "We have more secrets than we should."

Her lashes dropped, but not before he saw the hurt in her blue eyes. Without another word, she walked away, her hem leaving a trail in the white marble dust that coated the ground.

Charlotte stared into the dark corner of the workroom where a fire crackled in an iron stove. She didn't know what to think of this man. Everything about him confused her. He was ambitious, passionate, determined, and creative. His eyes glowed when he spoke of his family, his face suffused with a warmth that made him look young and approachable. But in the blink of an eye, that warmth would flee and all that would be left in its place was a mixture of icy fury and passion so hot she could sometimes taste it.

Ever since their conversation in the dining room, she'd found herself wanting to know more about him, the work he did, and why he did it. Whether she was chatting with Aunt Verity, riding in the forest on Angelica, or abed waiting to fall asleep, a thousand questions about this man would drift through Charlotte's mind, refusing to leave until they were answered.

She'd asked him some of those questions a few minutes ago, and his answers had been as interesting as she'd expected. But there were more things she wanted to know. What was Italy like? What countries had he seen? Did he ever travel with his brothers or sisters? What was the life of a sculptor like? Did he love it? Hate it? Were there things he'd change?

But the truly unsettling thing about her curiosity was that the more she knew about Marco and his life, the less satisfied she was with her own.

She would soon be married, her duty limited to her husband, his life, and eventually their children. Meanwhile, this man who even now watched her from across the room with a gaze so intense that she could feel it, was accomplishing something that would be treasured for centuries, something that would inspire others with its beauty, something that could bring joy well past his lifetime.

Charlotte's life was missing something, a fact which had become even more painfully obvious after Caroline died. For years before that fateful day, Charlotte had been restless and unsatisfied, but she'd told herself that she had plenty of time to find whatever it was she was supposed to do and be. Caroline's death had rudely ripped that falsehood away.

Now Charlotte knew the brutal unpredictability of life. Of the need to grab with both hands every experience and adventure that offered itself, and to savor them for all they were worth.

But how could she do any of that without turning her back on Robert, her family, her home here at Nimway? Were there adventures awaiting her that she'd never have if she continued to only do what was expected of her?

She had no idea, but while she searched for answers, the least she could do was take the time to learn what she could from the fascinating man now standing before her.

Charlotte slipped him a glance from under her lashes. "We have an excellent library here at Nimway."

He raised his brows. "I assumed as much."

"There are many, many books, and I happened on one quite by accident called *Methods of Sculpting*." She searched his face. "Have you heard of it?"

"Of course. It is a notable tome."

"Last night, when I was having trouble sleeping, I read some of it." Seven chapters, to be specific, a fact she wasn't planning on sharing.

"Did you learn much?"

"A few things. I now know what a tooth chisel is."

His mouth twitched. "Impressive."

The warmth in his eyes encouraged her to add, "I read something about a 'riffler,' as well. Those are used for smoothing, in case you didn't know."

"I know." His mouth curved into a smile, his dark eyes gleaming.

She added helpfully, "You may borrow the book, if you'd like. When I'm done, of course. Just in case you need to refresh your memory."

He laughed, the sound rich and deep. And she smiled in return, as happy as if she'd accomplished a miracle.

"Come." He pushed himself from the table. "You wished to see the work I've already done."

"Yes, please."

He walked past her to the far end of the workroom and she followed. Squares of sunlight shone onto the ground from the windows, white dust swirling at their feet. He stopped by several large slabs of creamy white marble that leaned against a wall.

"You brought these with you?"

"Yes. You must crate them carefully, but it can be done."

"They're beautiful," she said truthfully. She reached out to touch the marble, but he grasped her wrist, his fingers warm against her skin.

"Fine marble can soak in oils, and as you've been wearing gloves that have been tanned, then your touch could yellow the surface."

She hoped he couldn't feel her galloping pulse under his fingers. "I won't touch them."

"Thank you." He released her wrist. "I'll seal this piece before I install it, and then it won't be a concern. But for now, the stone must be protected."

"It's beautiful marble, so white but with traces of blue and gray."

"In certain light, it will gleam as if lit from within. This marble is mined from quarries near my home in Tuscany, near the town of Carrara." Satisfaction warmed his tone. "The Romans mined these quarries for centuries, and it's been said that Michelangelo himself used this marble for his most important works."

"Are there many types of marble? I haven't gotten to that chapter in the book."

He sent her an amused look. "There are more types, colors, and textures than you can imagine."

"My father says there a quarry near London that produces a

pale orange marble. He is not fond of it, although the Duke of Buckingham was, and has it displayed all throughout his new house."

"Taste does not come with money." He nodded to the corner where a large tarp hid something. "Here's the work I've finished." He tugged the tarp away to reveal several large, carved marble pieces. He nodded to the largest one. "This is the header. It goes directly under the mantel."

The header was a large, thick marble rectangle, a set of figures carved in the center that were Greek in design. To each side he'd added a thick swag of entwined wheat. The detailing was exquisite, and she was instantly awed by it.

"It's beautiful." She tucked her hands behind her back to keep from running her fingers over the smooth figures. "How long did this take you?"

"Weeks. The smaller figures take more time as one wrong tap and it could be ruined."

"It's beautiful and much larger than I expected. Will it fit?"

"Easily," he said. "The trim panels are substantial and will fill out the rest of the space."

"Are those done, too?"

"Yes. And so is the mantelpiece." He pulled aside more tarps, revealing the thick mantelpiece, which was thick and heavy but elegant, with masterful crenelated edge. Next to it were two smaller panels decorated with a delicately carved rope braid.

"These are the trim panels, I take it?"

He nodded. "They go to each side of the fireplace, between the fire box and the pillars, which I'm working on now."

She leaned forward to peer closely at the carvings. They were so perfect, so lifelike. "Robert Adams couldn't do better," she said honestly.

"Adams? Pah. There is no originality in his work."

"I'll make a note of that in the margin of my book. Sadly, the author seems to think him a god of some sort."

"Then the author is a fool," Marco declared. He picked up the discarded tarps. "Have you see enough?"

"Oh yes. My mother will be pleased." How could she be otherwise?

"Good." He threw the cover back over his work.

"What should I tell my mother about the pillars?"

"They will be near life sized and wonderful to behold," he said shortly. "That is all she needs to know."

He was so preemptory in his tone that she made a face and he laughed, his eyes crinkling. God, but she loved to make him laugh. When he laughed, her heart lifted. It was as if they were connected in some way.

Stop it, she told herself, frustrated with her wild thoughts, and somewhat amused, too. *This is what happens when you've spent too much time reading about the art of sculpture and too little time on sleep.*

Perhaps the truth of the matter was something simpler than mere tiredness. He was quite handsome, this dark-haired Italian. He should be modeling for statues, not making them. Normally, she wasn't swayed by such things. In fact, she'd never been swayed by any man, including Robert.

The reminder of Robert gave her pause. Yesterday, she'd finally received a note from him, one that was longer than a line or two. In three short paragraphs, he mentioned that he'd been busy meeting with his solicitor over matters of his estate, had bought a new horse with a fine gait, and that he would arrive at Nimway in two short weeks. As an afterthought, he'd added that he looked forward to seeing her.

At few weeks ago, a longer missive would have eased her doubts and assuaged her lonely heart. But now she wanted more and although longer, the note had been highly impersonal, the tone more fitting for a distant cousin than a lover.

Still, despite his shortcomings, Robert was her fiancé and she owed him her loyalty. She was no brazen flirt, and yet here she was, staring into the dark, mysterious eyes of a wildly handsome

Italian sculptor for no other reason than she was madly curious about his untamed, romantic life.

And that was what she so desperately craved, she reminded herself – she didn't want him, but his life of adventure and passion.

His brows rose. "*Scusi.* Do I have dust on my chin?"

Oh dear. I've been staring far too long. "No, no. I was just—" She clamped her lips closed and shook her head. "Thank you for sharing your work. It's far more beautiful than I could have imagined. But . . . I should return to the house now as my aunt will be waking from her nap soon."

His sensual mouth curved into a faint, lopsided smile. "If I had to have a chaperone, I would want one who naps, too." His eyes glinted wickedly and she found it difficult to swallow.

This man made her breathless, as if seeing him might, in some way, be wrong. Forbidden. It had been so long since Charlotte had tasted that particular freedom, of doing what she wanted for no reason at all other than it appealed to her, that she was almost giddy. *How I have changed.* As Aunt Verity had pointed out, all of the Harringtons suffered from that particular flaw, the desire to taste the forbidden. *All of us except Caroline. Caroline was perfect. Caroline had been everything good in this life, even—*

A large, rough hand gently cupped Charlotte's face and, shocked speechless, she looked up into Marco's eyes.

His smile was gone, his brows lowered as he whispered, "Every so often, I see in your eyes a sadness so deep it seems that it would swallow you whole."

"You can see that?"

"How could I not?" He slid his hand from her chin to her cheek, his thumb brushing her skin. "I cannot not bear to witness your pain."

Tears clogged her throat. She wasn't going to tell him her tragedies. She'd already revealed far too much. And yet, when she opened her mouth to deny him, other words slipped out. "My sister—" She couldn't say it, her throat as frozen as a pond in the deepest of winters.

His expression, already gentle, softened. "She is no longer with us." He didn't ask, but merely made the statement.

It was such a relief that Charlotte managed to nod without letting a single tear fall. "She died eleven months ago."

His thumb smoothed over her chin. "So that's it. She is gone, and you suffer."

"I'm getting used to it." Charlotte refused to think of those first weeks when she'd been so raw with pain. "Now, I'm . . . waiting."

"For what?"

For this. The thought caught her by surprise. In the months since Caroline's death, Charlotte had tiptoed around her parents' grief until her own pain had been lulled to sleep. But now those feelings stirred, bringing back her old restlessness as if she been waiting for something, or someone, to awaken them.

Was this what she'd been waiting for? For this man? This moment? This *feeling.* One she'd never experienced before. Longing and lust, desire and excitement. But it was more than that. It echoed something she'd thought she'd forgotten, that of being *alive.*

His gaze narrowed. "What is it?"

She locked her gaze with his and stepped closer. "I think . . . I think I might have been waiting for you."

He looked so astounded that she thought he might turn and walk away. But instead, with a muttered curse, he slipped his arm around her waist and pulled her against him, engulfing her in a heady warmth.

It wasn't a kiss, but a hug. She was surrounded by his strength, her head cradled on his chest as his heart beat steadily against her ear. It was heavenly, and she slipped her arms about his waist and closed her eyes, soaking him in.

"You fit into my arms far too well, little one," he murmured against her temple, his breath warm on her skin.

Charlotte burrowed deeper as she breathed in the smell of ink, paper, and warm stone.

Oh Caroline. If you could see me now. Charlotte smiled against Marco's soft shirt, thinking about how scandalized Caroline would have been. Caroline, who'd never had the least urge to do anything other than what was right and proper, and had lamented that Charlotte spent far more time in trouble than out.

The old Charlotte, the one she'd so carefully packed away after Caroline's death, had loved doing the forbidden. It had made her heart race, sent her blood thundering through her veins, and had made her feel alive.

She felt alive now, tucked into the arms of a stranger, his heart thrumming steadily under her cheek, his warmth pocketing hers. It was tempting to stay here forever, but the outside world would not let her. Aunt Verity would arise soon, if she hadn't already. And who knew when Marco's servant would finish dallying with Cook and return with their lunch?

Collecting herself, Charlotte dropped her arms and reluctantly stepped away, feeling embarrassed and exposed in some way. "I'm sorry. I shouldn't have—"

"No. Don't." His dark gaze never left her face. "You have nothing to apologize for."

She tucked a stray lock of hair behind her ear, hoping he didn't notice how her hand trembled. "Then . . . thank you." Her voice was so husky, she didn't recognize it.

"The pleasure was mine."

She looked up into his face, searching his expression for she knew not what. "You have been so kind. I—" Impulsively, she lifted up on her toes and kissed his cheek.

It was a chaste kiss, meant only to express her gratitude. But the second her lips touched his stubbled cheek there was a long, silent moment. Neither moved, frozen in place, lips to skin.

And then, like a strike of a flint to a stack of straw, the flame burst into life and she grasped his shirt and pulled him to her.

He turned his head, his mouth ruthlessly covering hers as he slipped his arms around her and lifted her off her feet.

She barely noticed, she was so caught in the kiss, her arms tangled about his neck, her mouth opening under his, her body aflame as he—

Clunk.

Marco broke the kiss and looked over her head to the door and cursed under his breath. Without another word, he lowered her back to her feet and stepped away, his breath harsh. *"Dio,* I am a fool!"

Her mouth burning from his kisses, she struggled to say, "Who was it?"

"My servant was at the door." Marco raked a shaky hand through his hair and then cursed again. "He will hurry back to the kitchen and talk, and you'll be in trouble and I—" He clamped his mouth over the rest of his words.

Charlotte pressed her hand over her heart where it thundered against her ribs. What would Aunt Verity say, if she found out Charlotte had been caught in such a flagrantly improper embrace? She wasn't sure she wanted to know. Aunt Verity was the laxest of chaperones, but that might be too much, even for her.

Marco's gaze brushed over her, moving over her face and her fingers where they now trembled against her swollen mouth. His expression darkened. "This was a mistake."

His words were hard, and sharp edged. They struck her heart like bricks against a window, shattering and unforgiving.

"I must catch him before he reaches the kitchen. You must leave." His face dark, Marco strode to the table. He collected her hat and gloves and brought them to her.

She took them unthinkingly. "I'm sorry your servant saw us. I should never have—" She shook her head. "But it wasn't anyone's fault. It was a kiss, no more. I—"

"Go."

"But—"

"Go," he ground out, his mouth white. "And Charlotte?" His gaze burned into hers, and there was a hopeless bleakness to his face that stopped her from speaking. "Don't come back."

What was happening? She tried not to take his harsh orders to heart, but couldn't seem to stop. Her temper slipped, and she managed to say in a cool voice that only trembled a little, "You forget yourself. I decide whether to visit my own stables or not." She knew to stop there, but couldn't. "I am the mistress of Nimway while my mother is gone, and I don't answer to you. I will return tomorrow to see your work on the pillars."

"No, you won't. I'll send word when there is something to see, but do not expect it to be soon. It will be a week, perhaps longer. Until then, you are not welcome here."

She bit her lip to keep it from quivering. Goaded by his flat expression, she said, "Fine. A week then. It's good it will take that long, for I've much to do. Far too much to come back here. I've a fitting tomorrow for my trousseau, and—and I've lunch with the vicar's wife, and that's just the beginning. I've got many, many other things – important things—on my calendar."

His expression had tightened as she spoke, and now his voice was cutting and cold. "We are both busy, it seems. Too busy to make a mistake like this again."

A mistake. Her eyes grew hot and her eyelids prickled. "Exactly. Now, if you'll excuse me, I'll leave you to your work." With a stiff curtsey, she swept out into the miserable sunshine, biting the inside of her lip to keep her tears at bay. It wasn't until she reached the house that she realized that, in addition to her pride, she'd also left the moonstone behind.

CHAPTER 7

The meeting with the dressmaker was as unpleasant as Charlotte had expected. Madame Guillemot was a thin, gaunt woman with a heavy, questionable French accent and a militaristic approach to fittings that would have made a general proud. Madame, ever punctual, arrived exactly on time with a retinue of harried looking assistants, young women who wore the same expressions as hunted deer. In addition to her harried servants, the modiste also brought twelve partially finished gowns, six pairs of new shoes, ten chemises made of spider-web fine lawn, numerous stockings and bonnets, hats and cloaks, and a dozen sheer night rails with matching peignoirs.

Overwhelmed by the rustle of lush silks and heavy brocades, Charlotte winced to think of the outrageous sums Mama was paying. The thought made Charlotte all the more determined to do her duty by the fitting, even though she'd have preferred to have a nail driven into her foot.

It didn't help that a few moments into the ordeal, Aunt Verity had whispered far too loudly that she rather thought Madame's accent was fake, for she sometimes forgot it all together. Thus, Madame was in a far from charitable mood when the time came for Charlotte to try on some of the more sumptuous ball gowns. The modiste tugged and pinned, poked and prodded, and repeatedly hissed, "Stand still!" until Charlotte was ready to scream.

She was relieved when Aunt Verity decided she'd finally had enough and told the woman that if she couldn't work with the fittings she had, then they would hire someone who knew how to use their time more efficiently. True to her charade, Madame had flown into a raging Gallic tirade where she'd brashly called Aunt Verity 'out of fashion.'

Up until then, Aunt Verity had seemed half asleep, but Charlotte soon discovered that her aunt did not suffer insults lightly. The second Madame paused for breath, Aunt Verity had answered, calling Madame every name in the book but polite. But as Verity had spun her tirade in pure, perfectly spoken French, Madame couldn't retort, for her atrocious accent and lack of vocabulary would have unmasked her.

The only thing Madame could do was retreat. Fuming, Madame had taken out her fury on her harried assistants, snapping at them until everything was packed back into their bandboxes and cloth sheaths. The assistants, their arms piled so high that they could barely see where they were going, hurried from the room while Madame, ever the actress, paused dramatically on the threshold. "Make no mistake; I will be writing to Mrs. Harrington about this outrage!"

"There's no need." Aunt Verity hid a yawn behind her plump hand. "Olivia will be home before a letter could reach her even if you knew where to address it."

Madame gasped, her mouth opening and closing like a fish thrown onto land. After a horrified moment, she spun on her heel and marched out.

Charlotte turned an admiring gaze on her aunt. "That was masterful."

"Thank you, my dear." Aunt Verity hooked a foot around the leg of a tasseled stool and pulled it closer. "I have no patience with pretenders, which is odd when you think of the fact I was once married to a fake baron."

"Uncle Albert wasn't a real baron?"

"Lud, no." Aunt Verity paused to kick off her slippers before she plopped her feet on the footstool, settling deeper into the settee. "My second husband was quite a charlatan, but he was charming, which goes a long way to making the unacceptable acceptable."

"But why did he lie about being a baron? Mama said he was quite well off."

"He was wealthy; he wasn't pretending about that. He just didn't inherit it as his father was a tailor."

"Where did Uncle Albert's money come from?"

Aunt Verity pursed her lips. "I don't know. We never really discussed it."

Charlotte burst out laughing. "Aunt Verity, you are the strangest creature! Did you know Uncle Albert wasn't a real baron when you married him?"

"Oh no. I didn't find out until a few months afterwards. But he was still the same man I'd married – funny, loving, charming. And then there was the money. You can't ignore that." Aunt Verity tugged her shawl a bit closer around her shoulders. "I loved him, you know. And he was mad about me. It's a falsehood to think that you can live with a person for years and know everything about them. Love never stops surprising."

"Mama knows everything about Papa."

Aunt Verity laughed. "Child, if you only knew! And don't ask me to tell you, for I will not. Your father would ring such a thundering scold over my head—" She shuddered. "Oh dear, I feel the need for some tea. Should I ring for it?"

"Yes, please." Charlotte wished Aunt Verity would tell her more about Papa. Charlotte had always suspected there was a great deal she didn't know about her father. He had the air of a man of mystery, even now.

Aunt Verity picked up the small silver bell that rested on the table beside the settee and rang it.

The door opened immediately, and a footman entered.

"Ah, Johnson! I know it's not yet tea time, but Miss Harrington and I just had a ghastly visit from a faux Frenchwoman and now we find ourselves in need of sustenance."

"I will bring a tea tray immediately, my lady."

"I knew there was a reason you have become my favorite footman. That would be lovely, Johnson. Thank you."

Smiling, he bowed and left.

Charlotte eyed her aunt. "You are trying to steal him, as well, aren't you?"

"I'm trying. Sadly, your servants are very loyal. You should be glad to know that."

Tea was brought in short order. Charlotte sent the footman on his way and poured the tea herself while Aunt Verity pulled herself into a more upright position on the settee.

Charlotte put two lumps of sugar into her aunt's tea and stirred it, the silver spoon clicking against the side of the cup.

Aunt Verity smothered a yawn. "Lud, but I am exhausted after that fitting."

"Me, too." She handed Aunt Verity her tea cup. "Every time Madame visits, I feel like a pincushion."

Aunt Verity sipped her tea, watching Charlotte over the rim. "Once the trousseau is done, you'll be one step closer to the wedding."

Charlotte picked up her cup of tea, ignoring her sinking heart. "Much closer." To be honest, ever since she'd left Marco in his workshop yesterday, she hadn't been able to muster enthusiasm for anything – not food nor sleep, but especially not thoughts of getting married. She was bound up in emotional knots, and she didn't know why. Was it merely doubts because of Robert's inattention? Or was it because she feared – no, she knew – she was developing a deep interest in Marco?

She caught Aunt Verity's sharp gaze and forced a polite smile. "My parents have been very kind in providing such a lovely trousseau. It's more than I expected."

"La, child. Your father can stand the nonsense. He's been very fortunate in his investments."

"Mama is quite proud of him for adding so much to the Nimway coffers. As much as she loves this house, it's expensive."

"Old houses are like men. They are going to cost you, one way or another, especially the ones worth keeping."

"True," Charlotte couldn't keep the sour note from her voice. In a remarkably short time, Marco had already cost her hours of sleep, a measure of her pride, and . . . well, other things, although right now she couldn't think of them.

Aunt Verity's gaze moved over Charlotte's face. "My dear, is something bothering you? You've been as blue as a megrim all day."

"I'm fine. There's just a lot going on right now and everything seems so complicated. When I agreed to marry Robert, I didn't realize it would be such a huge endeavor. I wanted a simple wedding, just enough to distract Mama."

Aunt Verity, who'd been in the process of putting a teacake on her plate, looked up and frowned. "Are you saying you're getting married just to give your mother a project of some sort?"

"Of course not, although I would be lying if I didn't point out that it has helped her. Between planning my wedding and redecorating, she's stayed busy and is much happier than she was in the weeks after Caroline died."

"Hm. Tell me, child, what are your plans *after* your wedding?" Aunt Verity ate a bite of cake, her sleepy gaze never moving from Charlotte's face.

Charlotte opened and then closed her mouth. What would happen after the wedding? *Good God, I hadn't thought of that. Not really.* She considered it a moment. "I suppose I'm to live with Robert in his home in London."

"I thought you weren't fond of the city. When I sponsored you and Caroline for your seasons, you said the city smelled of old eggs, and the people were cold and unfriendly, both valid observations, I should add."

Charlotte winced. "Did I say that?"

"You *and* Caroline said it." Aunt Verity looked regretfully at her empty plate. "Repeatedly."

"That's horrid. You should have smacked us for being so ungrateful."

"You were merely being honest. The streets of London smell horrid, some worse than others, and the people can be quite cold and unfriendly, especially if they think they are superior in some way." Aunt Verity put her empty plate on the table and reclaimed her tea cup and saucer. "But we were talking about your coming marriage, not your unfortunate season."

Charlotte laughed. "It was an unfortunate season, wasn't it?" Two years ago, when she and Caroline had been seventeen, Aunt Verity had sponsored her and Caroline for their first – and what turned out to be – their only season. They'd been presented at court and had attended a whirlwind of balls and dinner parties. They'd met dozens of eligible men, all of whom were madly in love with Caroline and painfully polite to Charlotte. "I never understood why Caroline demanded to end our stay in London and return home when she did."

"And after only three months! She was the bell of the season, too, a position most girls that age would die for." Aunt Verity lowered her teacup. "Charlotte, did you know your sister received no less than three proposals in the short time you were in London?"

"*What?*"

Aunt Verity muttered something under her breath. "I vow, but I must have told them a hundred times that you deserved to know."

"Them? My mother and father?"

"And Caroline. They feared you'd feel slighted."

"I wouldn't have. I'd have been happy for her."

"Of course you would have been. You don't have a selfish bone in your body."

A flicker of irritation made Charlotte say rather sharply, "They are always trying to protect me, and it's not necessary."

"True. You do quite well for yourself. Neither you nor Caroline ever lacked for strength of character. She could be quite opinionated, although in a polite, modest-seeming way."

"Papa always said she was quietly stubborn, while I was loudly stubborn."

"A very good description." Aunt Verity pursed her lips. "You know, I was surprised Caroline didn't accept any of her suitors, for they were all wealthy, well born, and of the peerage. One of them is now a duke. But she turned them all down."

Charlotte shook her head. "Caroline never told me." How had she kept such a thing secret? "Perhaps that explains why she wished to return home so suddenly. Perhaps it became too much."

"She didn't 'wish' to return home. She demanded it."

"Oh, I remember," Charlotte said with a smile. "She refused to attend another event. Mama was quite unhappy about it."

"I always thought your sister would have enjoyed her season more if she'd had a little less success. I believe at times she felt like a rabbit in the middle of a pack of hungry wolves." Aunt Verity sighed and looked around the room. "Your sister loved this house. She glowed whenever she spoke about it."

"It made her so happy. The week before Caroline died, she awoke me in the middle of the night. She'd had a bad dream that she'd left Nimway and couldn't find her way back. She was shaking and teary, and I let her sleep in my bed. In the morning, she was much better, but she seemed sad after that. As if the dream lingered."

"Poor dear. And then a week later, in the middle of the night, she packs a bandbox and rides off to do God knows what, only to meet a tragic end. None of it makes sense." Aunt Verity sighed. "I wish we might find your sister's diary. It would answer so many questions."

"We've looked everywhere for it, but there's no trace of it." Charlotte looked out the window where the sunshine glittered on the surface of Myrrdin Lake. The lawn waved in the breeze, colorful flowers nodding from where they'd been planted around the water's edge. Beyond the lake, the harvest gold field rippled as if a giant's hand gently stroked the bobbing heads of grain. Meanwhile, in the distance sat mysterious and beckoning Balesboro Wood. It was so beautiful here at Nimway, the only home she'd ever known. *Caroline, why were you leaving? And without a word, too. I don't understand.*

"Do you know else what I wonder about?" Aunt Verity helped herself to another tea cake. "Caroline had to know she'd receive offers while in London. I mean, that is the purpose of a season, so why did she find that very thing so taxing that it sent her running home?"

"Perhaps she just wanted the fun of visiting London, and going to balls, and seeing the sights, and – well, all of it. At first, she enjoyed herself so much. She met interesting people, saw the theater and the park, and danced until her feet hurt." Charlotte smiled. "Robert once escorted us to a ball and even though he was standing with us in the receiving line, he didn't get one dance with her as she was mobbed the second she set foot in the ballroom. He was quite miffed about that."

"He's a good dancer."

"He is, indeed. I should know, for I danced with him at every event. My dance card wasn't as full and he was very kind." *He's a good man. I know that and should remember it. Yes, he's a horrid correspondent, but not everyone takes to the pen. But that doesn't make him a poor choice for a husband, does it?*

She stirred restlessly, pouring herself more tea even though her cup was still nearly full. At one time, she'd thought being 'kind' was enough of a reason to marry someone. But was it? If Robert was indeed the man she should be with, why did she kept finding herself in Marco's company? She bit her lip, thinking of the simple, platonic kiss on the cheek she'd given him which had turned into something much, much more. Something heated. Now that her pride had healed a bit, she knew he'd been right to send her away. They could not be alone.

But shouldn't she feel wanton desire when she thought about Robert? Wasn't that a part of marriage? All they had was friendship, and she feared it wasn't enough to carry a marriage through the years.

"You're thinking of Robert, I can tell, for you've lost every vestige of your smile." Aunt Verity set her half-eaten tea cake aside. "Your Mama would not approve of what I'm about to say, but I cannot leave it unsaid. I've been married a number of times. Five, if you're counting. Four, if you're not. That makes me an expert on the subject of marriage. If you've any doubts about this marriage, then say so. Your parents might be shocked at first, but they would understand, and – from what little I know of Robert – so would he. He's always seemed a most pleasant man."

"He's a good person." Charlotte gave rueful smile. "Too good for me, I sometimes think."

"Nonsense. Although to be honest, I was surprised when your Mama told me he'd offered for you. Not because I don't think you're beautiful, because you are, but because after Christmas the year before last, I was certain he was—Oh *my*!" Aunt Verity's gaze, which had absently followed a streak of sunlight to one of the large windows, was now locked on some distant point outside.

She blinked. Once. Twice.

She flushed as she slowly stood, her hand stealing to her throat. "That's . . . oh dear."

What on earth? Charlotte stood, too. Still holding her cup of tea, she leaned to one side and peered around her aunt to see what was so intriguing.

There, walking along the path from the lake to the stables was Marco. He'd apparently gone for a swim, for his hair was wet, his white shirt – usually so loose – clung to his wet shoulders and broad, muscular chest. The sleeves were rolled back to his elbows, his powerful arms visible even from this distance. The sunshine lingered on him, outlining every well-defined muscle, the breadth of his shoulders, and the tight line of his stomach. Beads of lake water glistened as he reached up to rake back his wet hair, his muscles on fine display.

Charlotte's mouth was suddenly dry, and she absently lifted her cup to her lips but forgot to drink. He looked so—

Aunt Verity whirled to face her. "*No!*"

Charlotte blinked. "What?"

"You cannot look at that! And I, as your chaperone, will not allow you to!" Aunt Verity leapt between Charlotte and the window with a rustle of silk, holding her arms out in an effort to block the view. "Stop looking! Why, if your mother knew you'd seen that, she'd be furious with me."

Charlotte lowered her cup. "You were looking at him."

Under her powder, Verity's cheeks pinkened. "That's different; I'm not engaged to be wed. I may not be the strictest chaperone when it comes to your meandering about the estate on your horse, for I fail to see how you could be importuned on such a beast, but watching an almost nude male is another matter."

"He was fully clothed."

"It didn't *seem* like it, did it? Now come. You can sit in this chair over here, so the window won't be in your direct line of sight." She took Charlotte by the arm and led her to a chair facing the fire and gently pushed her into it. "I vow, but chaperoning is much more difficult than I imagined."

Aunt Verity returned to her settee, adjusted her skirt's panniers to each side, her neck quite flushed where there was no powder. After a long, awkward moment, she asked, "I don't suppose you know who he is?"

"He's the Italian sculptor Mama commissioned to make the fireplace in the dining room."

"He's Italian and an artist, too? Good God, what was your mother thinking? And now he's out there, wandering around with no clothes on."

Charlotte laughed. "Aunt Verity!"

"Fine, he was wearing clothes, but in such a way that one couldn't help but imagine what he must look like without them. That's not acceptable." Verity picked up her linen napkin and fanned herself. "And don't say that I shouldn't have looked, for I know it, but he was right there in plain view and I . . ." Aunt Verity's face softened as she leaned forward to say in a low tone, "As if anyone could help but look at such a man!"

"He's quite attractive."

"He is indeed. Women are in such a ridiculous place in the world. We aren't supposed to notice anything earthy, as if we were blind, deaf, and dumb, while men not only notice such things, but positively delight in it. It's so unfair."

"It's the same with my riding. I may ride all I want so long as I never gallop, never jump a hedge, never do anything but creep along at the pace of a slug on a perfectly flat surface."

"Society has not been fair to the fairer sex," Aunt Verity agreed, still fanning herself. "But to get back to this sculptor. What do you know about him?"

"I only know a little. He's Italian and he's gaining a reputation as a master sculptor. His father is a famous painter who no longer paints because of his health."

Aunt Verity's gaze had sharpened. "So. You've spoken to him, and at length if you know about his family."

"What? Oh no, not at length," Charlotte lied, hoping her cheeks didn't appear as flushed as they felt. "Mama asked me to report on his progress on the fireplace. She wants it finished in time for the wedding."

"So your mother tasked you with keeping an eye on him." At

Charlotte's nod, Aunt Verity dropped her napkin back into her lap. "Lud! Sometimes I wonder about your mama. She's far too smart to make such an error."

"He's not an error. He's quite famous in Italy."

"Oh sweetheart, I am famous in Italy and I'm not a sculptor."

"What are you famous fo—"

"La, child, how you talk!" Aunt Verity said in a rush. "I will speak with your mama when next I see her. In the meantime, you, my dear, must stay away from that man."

"But the fireplace—"

"He can write, can't he? Let him send you notes of his progress. That's all you need. In the meantime, you can put your energy into your other duties."

"What other duties?"

"Surely over the last year you've overtaken some of the responsibilities here at Nimway?"

"Mama trained Caroline to oversee the house. Except for basic housekeeping, I was never included. I'll never be a guardian of Nimway Hall, you know."

"But . . . why not?"

"Because I don't have the mark."

"The what?"

"The guardian is born with an oval mark on the back of her shoulder."

Aunt Verity looked horrified. "Do you mean to tell me that the ownership of this magnificent house rests on a happenstance *birthmark*?"

Charlotte nodded. "It's been that way for centuries."

Aunt Verity glowered. "And you don't have this mark, so – Bloody hell."

"Aunt Verity!"

"I know, I know, it's rude to curse, but *really*."

Charlotte smiled. "It never bothered me that Caroline was to have Nimway, because it felt right, in some way. Besides, I've always thought it would be exciting to travel. I'd hoped Robert and I might go abroad for our honeymoon, but he doesn't travel well. Both coaches and ships make him ill."

"Child, you are indeed a Harrington. We all suffer from wanderlust. In his day, your Papa loved to travel so much that vowed he'd never settle down." She laughed softly, her gaze focused on an image from the past. "One time, he even sho—Oh. Wait. I'm not to share that. Never mind."

"Aunt Verity, please! I know Papa was very different before he married Mama, but he won't talk about it."

"He will, one day. In the meantime, he won't thank me for spilling his secrets."

"He won't tell us anything, and now Caroline will never know." The thought of Caroline not being here to share that information, something they'd wondered about together since they'd been old enough to realize their father had a past of some sort, made Charlotte's heart ache. "Her death has changed everything. People never tell you that when a sibling dies, your place in life instantly changes. You're no longer the oldest, or the youngest, or the only. Both John and I felt it. But I was no longer a twin. That always made me feel special, and with her, I was never alone. When Caroline left, she took that with her, too."

"My dear Charlotte, I know you'll always miss your sister. No one can fix that. But no matter what, you are still you, our wild and untamed Charlotte."

"Wild and untamed." Charlotte had to laugh, though the sound was bitter. "Mama has spasms if she thinks I'm behaving in either of those ways. She doesn't want to lose another daughter."

Aunt Verity's sharp gaze didn't waver. "You cannot change yourself just to please others."

"I'm just trying to be better."

"Better implies that you weren't good enough before, and you were. You must be true to yourself, whatever you do. And if this marriage is what you would do if Caroline were still here, and you're certain you love Robert, then by all means, get married. But if you're merely trying to distract your mama with a wedding, or you think to become whatever it is you believe Caroline was to your parents, then you are making a grave error, one that will only end in great unhappiness for both you and Robert."

Good God, was that what she was doing? Was she trying to take Caroline's place? Charlotte looked at the delicate teacup where it rested on the table and wondered what she'd be doing if Caroline were still alive. Whatever it was, Charlotte doubted her plans would include Robert. *What does that mean?* She was afraid she knew the answer all too well.

Aunt Verity tsked. "Look what I've done! I've upset you horridly. See what happens when I'm made to become a chaperone – something I am *not* qualified for, besides being too young – only to be distracted by a handsome man? I start lecturing like a strict governess on every topic possible!" She patted Charlotte's knee and said in a pleasing tone, "Let's talk about something more pleasant. Tell me, what did you think of the blue silk gown? I do believe that was my favorite." Aunt Verity, always ready to talk fashion, went off into raptures over some of the materials and stitches they'd seen, while Charlotte absently nodded, sinking into her own thoughts.

What had her aunt meant by 'being true' to herself? Perhaps, had she been older when Caroline died, Charlotte would have known who she was. But when tragedy struck, she'd been in the process of figuring that out. How did she begin that journey again? She wasn't sure, and she desperately wished she knew. Lately, she'd only felt like herself when she'd been with one person.

Aunt Verity helped herself to more tea, and Charlotte took the opportunity to pretend to sneeze into her kerchief, which required her to turn her head toward the window. She managed to sneak a look at where they'd seen Marco walking from the lake, but he was long gone.

Disappointed, she tucked her kerchief back into her pocket and poured herself more tea. Aunt Verity had forbidden Charlotte to see Marco again, which irked. It was unlike her easy-natured aunt to do such a thing, but Charlotte supposed it was understandable considering Marco's bold masculinity, which was as fascinating as it was shocking.

Still, the more Charlotte thought about the unfairness of such a restriction, the more the wanted to challenge it. Why *shouldn't* she see him? She was no child, and she was quite able to take care of herself. True, she'd allowed her guard to slip in the past, which had led to some impulsive embraces, but that was only more reason for her to see him again, to regain control of such improper yearnings. Seeing Marco again would be good for her. Even Aunt Verity would agree, if she were thinking straight. But of course, who would think straight after seeing Marco like *that*?

Aunt Verity paused in her one-way discussion of the merits of silk wool to combed wool, her voice slower as she yawned between words.

Charlotte set her tea cup back on the table. Marco would be in his shop by now, working. She wondered if he'd made progress on the fireplace pillars. *What does he have planned for those? I would know already if he hadn't ordered me to stay away.*

That made *two* people who'd ordered her to avoid Marco's workshop. Charlotte's irritation increased, and she kicked absently at her skirts where they tangled around one of her feet. *I should have told him that I would visit him whenever I wanted, no matter what he said.* At one time, she'd have done just that and never given it a thought. But now . . . she frowned. Now it seemed wrong to be anything other than meticulously polite, even at the expense of her own thoughts and instincts.

She bit her lip, shocked at the realization. *Good God, Aunt Verity was right; I have changed.* Charlotte had been trying her best to make her mother and father happy, to follow in her sister's footsteps and be – well, the good child. She'd tried so hard that she'd actually done it, never realizing what she was giving up.

She couldn't be both sedate and lively, both quiet and loud, both perfectly behaved and wildly passionate. *I can't be both Caroline and Charlotte. I can only be me.*

A gentle snore pulled Charlotte's attention to her aunt, who was now snoozing peacefully, her empty teacup resting in her lap under her relaxed hand, her shawl puddled on the floor near her feet.

Charlotte smiled and carefully retrieved the forgotten teacup. She placed the china cup back on the tray and then collected the dropped shawl and spread it over her snoring aunt. "Thank you," Charlotte whispered, warmed by gratitude. "You don't know how glad I am you came."

The older woman snorted in her sleep, and then resumed snoring, looking adorably peaceful.

Charlotte kissed Aunt Verity's powdered cheek and then tiptoed out of the room, closing the door behind her.

In the hallway, she caught sight of Simmons speaking with two footmen. He dismissed them and hurried to join her. "Ah, miss. There you are. I take it Lady Barton is asleep?"

"Just now."

"I will awaken her. She'll be much more comfortable in her own bed chamber. I'll let Miss Hull know that her ladyship is on her way up to—"

"No, thank you."

The butler frowned. "But Lady Barton—"

"Leave her as she is." Charlotte ignored Simmons's shocked look and added, "There's no need to send word to Miss Hull. Lady Barton will stay in the sitting room and will enjoy her nap to the fullest." Every word Charlotte spoke seemed to free her a little more. "Aunt Verity is quite comfortable on the settee."

"But—"

"Leave her. If my aunt – or anyone else for that matter –

wishes to nap on a settee in the sitting room in the middle of the day or at any other time, then they should be left alone to do so. Do you understand, Simmons?" She didn't raise her voice, but instead favored him with the undaunted look she'd seen her mother use a thousand times before.

He flushed. "Yes, miss." He spoke stiffly and looked as if he'd swallowed a lemon.

"Post a footman by the door so Lady Barton isn't disturbed."

"Of course, miss. Will . . . will that be all?" He looked almost afraid of what she might say.

She thought for a moment, her gaze locking on the warm gold ring that encircled her finger. *What would I do, and who would I be, if Caroline was still here?*

And like that, Charlotte knew. Perhaps she'd known all along, but her spirit had been too wounded by her sister's death to listen. "Simmons, please bring some fresh ink to the library. I've letters to write. Two, in fact."

Simmons bowed. "Yes, miss. I'll see to it right away."

By the time the butler had fetched a fresh pot of ink from where it was kept locked in a cabinet in the pantry and had carried it to the library, Charlotte was already sitting behind the desk, her hands folded in front of her, ready to compose two of the most difficult letters she'd ever written.

CHAPTER 8

The muse came to him in the dark hours of the night, whispering him awake with a clarity of vision that had him stumbling from his bed, yanking on his breeches, and reaching for his tools before he was properly awake. He did as he always did when the muse came and let the image flow from his mind to his fingers without question, without pausing to consider anything but the feel of the marble giving away under the sharp edge of his chisel.

In his dream, for the first time, he'd clearly seen the two figures that would hold up the mantelpiece. No longer were the goddesses shadowy and distant. The caryatids would be rounded of face and limb, their outer arms and knees bent to add dimension. Neoclassical in design, bold in simplicity, they would wear elegantly draped togas, with jewels set into the leather of their sandals, and a smooth, shimmering whiteness on their arms, calves, and breasts. The togas, thin and revealing, would show more than they covered, baring one breast before hanging over their bodies, clinging to every curve.

It would be a masterpiece. He knew it even as he chiseled the rock, freeing the figures he could now visualize so clearly. He could see everything but their faces, although he knew those would be revealed in time. For now, he would work the bodies, the limbs, the folds of the togas, the details of their sandals. *So much to do.*

And so he worked, and then worked some more. The marble gave way under his fingers, confirming that his design was exactly what it should be. Marble chips piled on the floor at the feet of the pillars as sweat beaded his brow, but he continued on. He ignored the dust clinging to his skin, pausing only to wipe the sheen from his forehead when his eyes began to sting.

When he finally stopped, the dark of night had slipped into the brightness of sunrise. He set his chisel and hammer aside, his arms and shoulders aching from his efforts. Too awake to return to bed, he found a stool and pulled it in front of the figures and sat there, evaluating what he'd accomplished.

Shortly after the sun had cleared the horizon, Pietro appeared in the doorway, his white hair rumpled, one side of his face creased to match his now-abandoned pillow. He scratched his ass as he approached. "The muse returned, did she?" Pietro eyed the marble chips piled at the foot of the pillars. "Did you get any sleep?"

"Some." Marco crossed his arms and looked at the stone with satisfaction. "I know everything but the faces. Those I could not see."

"You saw the rest of clearly enough." Pietro ran a practiced eye over the shadowed outlines. "The drape of those togas will be something to behold when you finish."

Marco nodded, pleased Pietro could already tell so much. "When they are done, they will capture the eye and never let go." He stood, moving from side to side to examine the roughed in figures from various angles.

This was the part he enjoyed the most, watching the figures emerge from the stone. The muse had done her work well, he decided with satisfaction. What joy he found in his craft. Anyone could be taught to carve stone, to polish it until it shone. But it took hard work, a sometimes painful struggle, and a deep, abiding patience to find what was hidden within the stone.

"How long will it take you to finish?"

He thought of how much progress he'd made last night. "A week, perhaps a day or two more. Then the marble must be polished until it shines."

"I can help with that when the times comes. You are well on your way, my friend." Pietro gave the sculpture another admiring look and then yawned, stretching his arms over his head, his back cracking loudly. When he finished, he collected his shoes from where he'd left them beside one wall, and tugged them on. "I'm off to the kitchens to see what's to be had for breakfast. Should I bring you something?"

"No. I want to rinse off this dust, and then sleep. I'll eat later."

"You're not going to take another bath in the lake, are you?" Pietro shook his head and said in a sour tone, "You'll thin your skin until it can no longer protect your blood."

"The Romans believed baths were healthy."

Pietro snorted. "Romans," he scoffed. "What do they know?" With that sally, he yawned and shambled toward the stable door, stopping just inside to send Marco a sharp look. "I hope I don't return to find you holding the daughter of the house again."

"I will not see her," Marco said shortly. "I've already told you that."

"That's what you said the last time, too."

"The last time, I had not so rudely dismissed her. She will not speak to me now, nor do I blame her." He'd been brutal, but he'd had to, for his own sake as well as hers. Still, her hurt expression haunted him.

Pietro shook his head. "You are a stubborn fool, but I suppose I must trust you."

"Go to the kitchen before Cook decides to give your breakfast to a handsome footman who is not such a horrible pain in the morning."

The stonemason grinned. "No footman can replace me. But still, I'm hungry, so I'll go."

"Good. When you do, deliver that moonstone to the butler. It's in the bag by the door. Tell him it was brought here by mistake."

Pietro grimaced.

Marco lifted a brow. "You don't like Simmons?"

"He thinks I spend too much time in the kitchens. Cook laughs at him, but I think he has an interest there and is jealous."

"It's more likely he hates seeing his winter stores depleted by an outsider, for you eat more than any two people I know. Now go, and don't hurry back. I've a wish to see my pillow before the half hour is done and you always make so much noise that I cannot sleep."

Unrepentant, Pietro took the moonstone and left, whistling a merry tune.

Marco returned to the pillars and crouched before them, examining his work inch by inch. He could see details he had yet to carve – the dimple in an elbow, the curve of a knee, the delicate folds of the togas.

He traced his fingers along the line of one shoulder, and realized the two figures had the same width. He stepped back and compared them, surprised to find them identical in every measurement. When he'd dreamed about the figures, he'd thought them sisters, but now he realized that they were representations of the same woman in different poses. She was magnificent, this creature. In his minds' eye, he could see the turn of her ankle, the delicate hollows that lay along her collarbone, the roundness of her arms, and the length of her curvaceous thigh. *When men see you, they will fall in love.*

He thought about working some more, but knew he was too tired and he dared not make a mistake. So instead, he found a clean rag and went out into the sunshine. Using the rag, he slapped the dust from his hair, shirt, and breeches. Shimmering and white, the marble dust swirled into the breeze and then disappeared, the distinctive scent mixing with that of fresh hay and morning dew.

When he finished, he tossed the rag back into his workshop and pulled his shirt over his head, and then strode behind the stables to the well. He tossed the shirt over a nearby shrub, and cranked up a pail of fresh, icy water. He poured the bucket over his head, gasping at the cold. It took several more buckets, but finally the water ran clear, the dust and sweat washed away. He used one last bucket of water to wash his shirt, wringing it out and tossing it over his shoulder.

Cold and wet, he rinsed the bucket and then hung it back in place and then headed back to the workshop, the thought of sleep beckoning. Despite his refreshing bath, his eyes blurred with tiredness.

As he turned the corner of the building, he stopped. Charlotte was in the center of the stable yard, perched on her horse, her high crowned hat shadowing her eyes as she bent down to say something to one of the grooms. The poor man stood near a mounting block he'd obviously brought for her use. He leaned forward, hanging on her every word, his manner ridiculously eager.

Marco tried not to scowl but failed. Truly, he couldn't fault the poor man. Charlotte looked especially beautiful today. Her hand rested gracefully on the pommel, her heart-shaped face softened by her smiles. She was indeed a goddess, Marco decided, too tired to stop himself. She was Diana of the Hunt, and he wished he could carve a statue of her right then and there.

She said farewell to the groom, and then straightened, seeing Marco for the first time.

Their gazes met, and locked. He waited for the flash of hurt anger he was sure he'd be met with. But instead, she favored him with a slow, faint smile, and then tipped her hat in his direction, her head tilted at a saucy angle.

He didn't know what to do; her reaction so at odds with his

expectation that all he could do was stare. Fortunately, she didn't wait for him to figure it out. As soon as her hand fell from her hat brim, she turned Angelica toward the fence surrounding the stable yard. With a gentle motion, she set the horse to a canter straight toward the fence, her skirts streaming alongside the horse's flanks.

Good God, she's going to jump that damned fence! Heart racing, Marco took a step after her. *What in the hell is she thinking? That fence is too high and there's a ditch beyond it!* Even worse, not only was she riding a brute of a horse, but she was riding sidesaddle, which he'd never trusted.

Before his horrified gaze, Charlotte urged Angelica to a faster pace as they approached the fence, the horse's long legs eating the ground as she thundered toward the fence and ditch.

Marco held his breath, his hands clenched at his sides.

Just before she reached the fence, Charlotte gathered the horse beneath her. At the last possible moment, they launched into the air and sailed over the top rail, the jump wide as they cleared the ditch and landed smoothly on the other side. Without a break in stride, they continued on, cantering easily toward the trail that circled the lake.

Marco exchanged a shocked look with the groom who still stood in the middle of the stable yard. "Does she normally do that?" Marco demanded

"She used to do it every day, but she hasn't made a jump like that since her sister's accident." The groom's gloomy face held a hint of admiration. "Miss Charlotte can ride, though. She hasn't taken a fall since she was a girl."

Marco joined the groom, watching Charlotte canter toward the lake. "I think I lost ten years of my life just now."

"See this?" The groom pointed to his own brown hair, which was thoroughly streaked with gray. "All of it comes from watching Miss Charlotte ride."

Marco laughed.

The groom gave Marco a measuring look and thrust out a hand. "Jimmy Davis."

Marco shook the man's hand. "Marco di Rossi."

"I know who you are. We all do. Some of us have taken a look at your work." The groom nodded as if he was a famous art critic. "You do well."

"Thank you," Marco said drily.

"You're welcome. It's been wonderful to see the improvements Mrs. Harrington has made to the house. I was born here, you know, as were most of us. The Harringtons are a good family."

"I just learned of Miss Caroline's death. It's tragic to hear of one so young dying."

Davis glanced over his shoulder and then moved slightly closer to say in a low voice, "The accident is not something we speak about openly. It was a tragedy and the family still grieves. But she was a lovely girl, Miss Caroline." He shook his head. "Although it's anyone's guess what she was doing riding a horse she barely knew, and in the middle of the night, too."

"So that's how she died."

"Something must have startled the horse, for it threw her. She wasn't found until the next morning when she didn't show up for breakfast. Her bed was found unslept in, and a search party was formed, but . . ." He sighed, his eyes shiny. "She was a lovely, kind girl, Miss Caroline."

"Where was she going so late at night?"

"Aye, that's the question, isn't it? No one knows. If you ask me, it's Balesboro Wood as did her in." The groom eyed the woods with suspicion. "Evil spirits lurk there."

"I don't trust those woods, either. The trails are impossibly difficult."

"'Tis the pixies. They find it funny to lead people astray, evil creatures." Davis sighed and picked up the mounting block. "I guess I'd better take this back inside. If you need anything, let me or one of the others know."

"Thank you. I will do that."

Marco watched as Davis disappeared back into the stables before turning back to where Charlotte was just disappearing into Balesboro. *So that is what happened to your sister.* He couldn't imagine how horrible that must have been, to have lost a sister at such a young age, and in such a way. If Davis was to be believed, there was still a mystery attached to the death, too. That would make it all the harder to accept.

He watched Charlotte until she was out of sight, glad the groom wasn't still here to witness Marco staring after Charlotte like a lovesick fool. Maybe he was imagining things, but there was something different about her today. When he'd met her in the woods that first day, she'd been stiff with caution. She was the opposite of the woman who'd just tipped her hat at him in such a bold manner, her eyes sparkling with amusement.

Shaking his head, he walked back to the workshop. He threw his wet shirt over a bench, found a towel, and dried his hair. With each tousle of the towel, his energy seeped away, his fatigue returned. He had to sleep. He gave the pillars a final look, and then went into his room where he stripped out of his wet breeches and fell into bed, falling into a deep sleep where marble caryatids, freed from the stone, danced with a woman with fire-colored hair who rode a horse made of snow.

CHAPTER 9

Two days later, deep in Balesboro Wood, Charlotte rode Angelica down random paths, some carved for horses, while others were little more than pathways fashioned by wild animals. The going was slow, but neither she nor Angelica cared. Overhead, the sun filtered through the branches, splashing onto leaves until they shone emerald and mint and every shade in between.

It was a luscious day, the sky a bright blue, the scent of spring heavy in the air and on the skin. She took a deep breath, sucking in the freshness of her beloved Balesboro. She loved these woods. She never felt safer than when she was here. It was both ironic and tragic that Caroline had died on one of these paths.

Charlotte shook away the thought, refusing to think about anything sad. It had been several days since she'd talked to Aunt Verity in the sitting room, and each day had brought Charlotte closer to where she was before the tragedy that had changed her life. She felt stronger and surer of herself now, and less as if she were walking on the egg shells of the expectations of others. With that came a peace she hadn't felt in months.

Angelica whickered softly, and then abruptly turned onto a path Charlotte didn't recognize. She allowed the horse to take the lead, for no animal knew the woods better, and sure enough, the pathway widened, the sound of rushing water lifting over the rustle of leaves. A few moments later, they entered a small clearing by a stream so picturesque that Charlotte pulled Angelica to a halt.

Before them, a wide stream bubbled over silvery moss that waved across copper colored stones. Clumps of blue and purple flowers grew entwined with emerald green grass. Overhead a gentle breeze rustled through the leaves, the sound merging with the rushing water. Even after all of these years, Balesboro still held some surprises and Charlotte was thoroughly charmed.

She patted the horse's wide neck. "Good girl."

Angelica whickered in return.

Charlotte glanced up at the sun and wondered if she had time to linger. She was due back at Nimway in an hour, for the vicar's wife was visiting and Aunt Verity had begged Charlotte to be there. If there was one thing Aunt Verity hated more than expending herself, it was exchanging small talk with a pious woman given to denouncing the very sins Aunt Verity enjoyed the most.

Charlotte grinned and then kicked the stirrups free. An hour would be better than nothing. With a lithe move, she slid off Angelica's back and looped the reins over a tree branch near a thick patch of grass. The horse settled in for a nap as Charlotte hung her hat on a shrub, and then went to the stream. A large outcropping of rock hung over a quiet pool, the stone surface invitingly smooth.

She bent down and placed her hand flat on the stone, pleased to find it warm. She sat on the rock and tugged off her boots, setting them to one side. She peeled off her stockings and tossed them over her shoulder so they would be well away from the damp stream. Barefoot at last, she pulled up her skirts over her knees, scooted to the edge of the rock, and dangled her bare feet into the pool.

Cool, fresh water rushed over her feet and she wiggled her toes happily. She only wished she had time to undo her cumbersome riding habit and swim in the quiet pool. But the memory of Aunt Verity's horrified expression when Charlotte had mentioned the vicar's wife killed the thought. *Another day then, if Angelica can be bribed into finding this place again.*

Humming to herself, Charlotte planted her hands behind her and tilted her face to the sun filtering through the branches. It had been three days since she'd had her conversation with Aunt Verity. Three days of solitary rides while she decided who she was, what she wanted, and all the reasons she shouldn't think about Marco di Rossi.

She wasn't sure what she should do about him. Her life was at a crossroads, and she was ready for something to happen. Something exciting. Something wonderful.

Something like him.

But no, she told herself, that something couldn't be him. She knew the price he'd have to pay if he 'crossed the line,' as he put it. And, as much as Charlotte hated to admit it, knowing her mother, there would be a price. Mama was loving and gracious to everyone she knew, but she had a will of steel and she always, *always* put family first. Charlotte had no illusions how her mother would see a flirtation between her daughter and the sculptor commissioned to make an unforgettable fireplace for the family home.

There was no winning this one. If she pursued him, or he her, which was a thrilling thought indeed, they both stood to lose. He could lose his reputation and career, and she would have hurt her mother's already tender feelings in a way that might never heal.

Charlotte sighed and closed her eyes, letting the sun warm her face. It was a problem, this fascination she had for Marco, but she couldn't seem to give it up. Not yet. There had to be a way around their problems, a way that would free them to at least explore the attraction that simmered between them. *Perhaps that would be enough to end it.*

Yet somehow, she doubted it. She kicked at the water and watched it arc into a line of splashes, each smaller than the first. She wished Caroline were here. She would have known what to do. There was nothing she'd like better than a romance, often said life wasn't worth living without—

Angelica snorted loudly, prancing nervously.

Charlotte turned to look. Somewhere close by, and coming closer, a large animal crashed through the shrubs. She started to rise, but the noise was instantly followed by a muttered curse in a deep voice she recognized far too quickly. Fighting a grin, she watched as Marco burst from a dense patch of shrubs, his face dark with irritation, a small branch caught in the torn shoulder of his shirt, a smattering of leaves tangled in his long, dark hair.

His saw her and surprise replaced his irritation. With a swift glance, he took in the beautiful pool, her tossed aside hat, her bunched skirts, and her bared feet dangling in the pool of water.

She waved. "Hello." It was a weak greeting, but she was too startled to do else.

He scowled, swiping at his hair, leaves showering down. "This cursed wood will be the death of me. If I find that damned owl, I'm going to throttle it and make a hat of it." With a disgusted look, he yanked the twig from the tear in his shirt.

"What owl?"

"The one I was chasing."

She tried to keep from laughing, she really did.

His lips thinned. "It's not funny. The damned thing swooped into the window while I was working, snatched up one of my sketches, and then flew off. I followed him to the woods just as he dropped the paper under a tree." Marco bent to dust his pants, pausing to yank a torn vine which had wound itself around his knee. "It wasn't very far inside the woods, so I thought it would be safe to retrieve it." He straightened, his brow lowered. "But when I reached the tree, the sketch was gone."

Fascinated, she asked, "What did you do?"

"I decided to return to my workshop, but the damned owl hooted at me. When I looked up, there he was, a little way farther into the woods, holding my sketch. I have no idea how he got it. I had my eyes on the paper the entire time, so—" He shook his head.

"Why do you think he took it? What would an owl do with a sketch?"

"Woman, how would I know what an owl was thinking?"

She bit her lip at his roar. When she could keep the laughter from her voice, she said, "You wouldn't know what an owl was thinking, of course."

"You're damned right I wouldn't. It makes no sense, but there he was. This time, I ran at him as fast as I could and leapt into the air and grabbed at the sketch. My fingers closed over it, but he was quicker and flew off." Marco scowled. "It was like he knew just when to take flight. I kept at it, but every time I reached him, he'd fly off, hooting at me, that damned sketch fluttering as if helpless."

"You continued to follow him."

"I did, like a fool. And we got deeper and deeper into the woods, too. Eventually, he disappeared, but it was too late by then, for I was good and lost. I've been wandering in these woods for nigh on two hours now and—Good God, woman, will you stop laughing!"

"Sorry." She gulped back another chuckle.

"No, you're not," he said grimly, although his eyes twinkled at bit. "I'm glad I found you. You *do* know how to get back to Nimway?"

"Yes, and so does Angelica."

"Thank God for that, at least. That owl hates me with a passion, and ... *Dio,* I sound mad, even to my own ears."

"Anyone who knows Balesboro would know you're not mad."

Marco thought he detected real sympathy in Charlotte's voice, which was infinitely better than the laughter that she'd so far showered him with. "Thank you." *I think.*

She turned back to the pool and gently slapped her feet on the water, smiling at the noise. "The villagers swear there's magic here. I've seen a few things that have made me believe it, too."

He walked to where she sat on the rock, looking around him as he went. He was struck by the beauty of the place, although as stunning as the water and trees and moss were, none compared to the vision in blue who even now was wiggling her toes in the still pool.

It was idyllic here, and yet he'd sworn he would stay away from her. But he was hot and tired, and the stream – and she – looked so inviting that he was pulled closer. "Have you truly seen magical things in these cursed woods?"

"Nothing any more at odds with reality than an owl luring you ever deeper into the woods. But yes, I've seen things." She pursed her lips, and he couldn't help but admire the fullness of them. "When Caroline and I were young, we played all through Balesboro. We saw lights that flickered, music playing where there were no instruments, and odd shadows that would flitter at the edge of your vision making you think you'd seen something impossible."

"If I saw or heard any of those things, I would run all the way back to Italy and never return."

She smiled and patted the rock on which she sat, her blue riding habit tucked around her. "Come and sit."

He shouldn't. He should go home and get back to work. But his knee had been sadly wrenched when he'd landed from his last leap at that blasted owl, and she looked so beguiling that he came and took his place on the warm rock, close to her.

Instantly, the world seemed better. All of his irritation, all of his fury, all of his worries about his work, even his torment over his feelings for Charlotte, was lured away by the warm rock. He patted it absently. "This is nice."

She smiled. "It is, isn't it?"

"It's *really* nice. And 'nice' isn't even a strong enough word." He considered it for a moment and then announced, "This is *blissful.*"

"You should take off your boots. The water feels wonderful."

"I'm fine just sitting, thank you." He tried not to look at her bared legs, and failed miserably, and could only be happy when she didn't notice. Her legs were just right, curved calves to fit a man's hands, ankles delicate enough to warrant further exploration. God, but she was a beautiful woman. It seemed he found her more so every time they met.

To distract himself, Marco looked up at the green trees swaying overhead. "People always talk about how green England is. I never understood that until I came here." He looked back at Charlotte, a wood nymph perched on a sun-warmed rock with hair the color of the sunset and eyes like the deepest night sky.

He leaned her way the slightest bit, his shoulder brushing hers. Pleased beyond belief when she didn't move away, he said, "Have you never been lost in Balesboro?"

"Never. I think these woods know and protect me."

"Yes, well, they torture the rest of us." He showed her one of his hands, which was streaked with scratches from brambles that seemed to grow out of nowhere as he'd lurched through what had seemed like a hundred walls of thorns.

She winced at the sight. "Oh dear." She reached into her pocket and pulled out a kerchief, and then bent down to dip it in the water.

"There's no need for that. I'll be f—"

She placed the wet kerchief on his hand, the pain instantly easing.

Well. That was something. "Thank you."

"You're welcome." She flattened the kerchief on his hand, and then left it there.

He instantly missed the touch of her hands on his. He watched her for a long moment, noting the gentle curve of her mouth, the usually peaceful feeling emanating from her. "You seem different."

She shot him a surprised look. "How so?"

"I don't know. Less . . . tense, perhaps. I like it," he said honestly. "You were rather prickly when we first met."

"Was I?" She wiggled her toes in the water. "Perhaps I was trying too hard to be something I'm not."

"Which is?"

She smiled. "When I was a child, I never did as I was told. One time, when I was about seven years of age, I got in an argument with Papa, who was angry with me for sneaking out late at night to visit the stables. He was right to be angry, you know, for it wasn't safe, but at the time, I thought he was being so unfair. I was so angry with him that I ran away. I packed my favorite doll, a clean chemise, and a pillow in a hatbox, stole an apple from the larder, and came here, to Balesboro."

"Seven years old and you came into these woods alone?"

"Yes." She laughed softly when he shook his head in disbelief. "I had the wild idea that I would live here until winter. By that time, my Papa would have decided he was very, very sorry for having been so stern with me, and would let me visit the stables whenever I wished."

"A lovely dream. But one apple wouldn't have lasted that long."

"Oh, it didn't last the hour, for I hadn't had my breakfast yet. But Balesboro seemed to know I wasn't yet ready to return home. I found berries and nuts, and I spent the whole day following a stream, chasing butterflies, and red song birds. I found a heart shaped rock that's still on my dressing table. Oh, and two bright blue feathers that I lost long ago."

"I'm surprised you bothered to go home."

A soft smile touched her mouth. "I might not have, but Caroline came for me, which wasn't easy for her, as she didn't like coming into the woods alone. I don't know how she found me, but she did. She said it was time to go back, so I went."

"Was your Papa cured of his irritation by then?"

"He was *very* happy to see me, but not as happy as I was to see him." She kicked at the water, the droplets flashing a faint rainbow over the green hazed rocks.

God, but he would love to sculpt her as she was now, her prim habit covering her to her neck, her rumpled skirts pulled up to reveal her delicate ankles and lush calves. He would call it Propriety In The Wild, he decided, drinking her with his gaze. "Why are you here? Are you angry with someone this time, too?"

She held her feet before her and pointed her wet toes, water dripping back into the pool. "I was thinking about Caroline." She kicked the water again, only not so gently. "I miss her."

The words, so simple, held a world of heartbreak. "That's understandable."

"She was to be the guardian, you know." Charlotte reached out and plucked a flower from a nearby clump and tucked it behind her ear. "Nimway Hall is always in the possession and care of a female of the line. My sister was to be the next one."

He shrugged. "So now it will be you."

"It can't be me. I don't have the mark."

"What mark?"

"Goodness, must I explain this to everyone? My aunt asked the same question." She slanted him a measuring look, as if she were deciding how much to tell him. He must have passed muster for she said in a serious tone, "Every guardian of Nimway is born with a mark on their shoulder, an oval. My sister had that mark. I don't."

"Do you wish you did?"

"Yes . . . and no. If I became the guardian, I'd need to stay here to oversee the care of the Hall. I'm not sure I want that."

"Won't you have to leave once you marry, anyway?" he asked.

"I suppose so."

She supposed? How could she not know? "Who is this man that you're to marry? What's his name?" The words burst from him, and he realized he'd been wondering about it since the moment she'd told him she was to marry.

"His name is Robert." She plucked another flower, holding the stem between her palms. She moved her hands slowly, rolling the flower back and forth. "I don't want to talk about him."

Neither did he, Marco decided. In fact, he couldn't think of anything he wanted to talk about less. Still, he was here. And so was she.

He steeled himself. "I've been here almost two weeks and I have yet to see this man."

She didn't answer.

"If you're going to marry this – what did you call him? Roberto?"

Her eyes narrowed. "Robert."

"Whatever it is. If you're going to marry him, then you'll be leaving Nimway, so you couldn't be the guardian, even if you wanted to."

She twirled the flower a little faster.

"That is, if he plans on taking you away. Perhaps he will want to live with you and your parents here."

The flower was almost a blur.

"Where is he now, anyway?"

She stopped twirling the flower and sent him a flat look. "I told you, I'm not going to talk about him."

Marco waited.

She sighed. "Fine. There's not much to tell, anyway. After we became engaged, he had business to attend to, and he left to take care of it."

"Business. What business is that?"

She didn't answer.

"He didn't tell you, did he? What sort of man—"

"Will you stop talking about him!" She glared, the flower a

ragged pulp in her clenched hand. She looked like a fluffed kitchen, her hair mussed, her feet bare, her hackles raised by his questions.

Marco covered her hand with his, the poor flower now hidden from sight. "If I were engaged to you, I would never leave you. When a di Rossi marries, it is for love and it is for life."

Something flashed in her blue eyes, but she turned away, shaking her head as if banishing cobwebs. "You don't understand."

"Try me."

She pulled her hand from his and threw the broken flower into the water. It floated in the quiet pool, swirling with the current.

They were silent, and it seemed that the forest was quiet now, too.

Marco hated that he'd crushed what had been a beautiful moment. *What in the hell is wrong with me? I could have sat here in this lovely grotto with this beautiful woman and talked about all sorts of things that might have pleased her.*

But that was the problem, wasn't it? He couldn't afford to please her. They didn't have the luxury of a leisurely courtship. If he didn't press for answers, then the time would come for him to leave and he'd never know what could have been.

What could have been. There were no sadder words in the world. He rubbed his knee where it still ached. "I shouldn't be talking to you about this man. I just . . ." He turned to her. "I don't understand why you are marrying him. If he doesn't care enough to stay with you, then he is not worth your efforts."

Her gaze searched his face, two more strands of hair falling from her coif to land on her shoulder. "You're being annoyingly persistent."

"I have to be."

"Yes, but I haven't even told my aunt this yet, and—" She gave an irritated sigh. "For your information – and I'm not sure why I'm telling you this – but I'm not going to marry Robert."

A surge of triumph flew thought Marco, shocking in its intensity.

Unaware of his reaction, she added, "I wrote him several days ago and told him so. He should get the letter tomorrow, perhaps the day after, but soon."

"I see." How could such news make him feel so elated? He had no idea, but there was no denying the blinding happiness that echoed through him. He had to breathe quietly for a moment before he spoke, or she'd have known it, too. "When did you decide this?"

"A few days ago."

"What happened?"

"My aunt said something that made me realize I was being unfair to both myself and Robert. That was one reason."

"There's another?"

Her gaze met his. "The last kiss we shared. I couldn't marry Robert after that. I just hadn't yet admitted it to myself."

"I'm glad you took this action." Incredibly glad. This wild, spirited woman deserved so much more than being trapped in a cold, English marriage. "You are too good for him."

"No, I'm not." She brushed some of her fallen hair from where it clung to the side of her neck. "He is too good for me."

Marco's smile faded. She didn't look at all pleased with her decision. In fact, she seemed very unhappy, her eyebrows knit, her teeth worrying her bottom lip. "You're worried you've hurt him."

She nodded. "I've known him since I was a child and he's always been kind to me."

"You would hurt him more if you married him and it wasn't supposed to happen."

"That's true." She straightened her shoulders and said in a firm tone, "It is for the best. He will come to see that soon enough."

She had such a tender heart, this one. And he liked her all the more for it. Marco had to fight the urge to sweep her into his arms for a hard kiss. God, but she was delectable.

She placed her hands flat on the rock behind her and leaned back, looking up at the trees. "Life is so complicated. All we want is to be happy, but no one knows what that really means."

"Love is happiness. I know that." Marco reached past her to pluck a flower. It was cornflower blue, the center a deep purple, the smell indescribably sweet. "In his time, my father painted hundreds of portraits of people, many of them wealthy beyond belief."

She watched him, her long lashes shadowing her blue eyes.

"He was in many different homes and saw many different people's lives. He says that of the houses he visited, he never once witnessed happiness close to the kind he and my mother shared." Marco dropped the flower in her lap where the petals rested on the folds of her skirts. "Not once."

She picked up the flower and looked at it. "True love is rare."

"Most people never get so much as a taste of it. But when they have it, they – and everyone around them – know it."

"My parents have that kind of love." She absently brushed the flower along her cheek. "You're right. They do know it, and if you saw them together, you would know it, too." She sighed, her breath making the flower flutter helplessly. "They will be upset when they find out I've ended my engagement."

"He will tell them?"

"I wrote my mother at the same time I wrote him. I thought it only fair." She dropped the flower back into her lap. "Mama has been worried about me since Caroline's death. I think she believed marriage would anchor me some way."

"If she thinks you need to be anchored, then she hasn't seen you when you're angry. You are a force, then. Even I fear you and I can pick you up with one arm."

A reluctant smile touched her lips. "I am forceful at times." She said it as if she'd just discovered it. "It's been a while since I felt I could be that way, or even honest, especially with my mother. She's been so sad since Caroline died." She turned her face to the sun, wincing when she noticed the angle of it. "It's getting late and I must return to Nimway. My aunt will be waiting for me."

To his chagrin, she climbed to her feet, her skirts dropping back to her feet, her bare toes peeping out from the folds.

Damn it. He didn't want this moment to end. He wondered if he could convince her to stay. Not just for a day, but forever. They could build a home of some sort here, beside this stream. He could set traps for food, and they could eat berries and nuts from the woods. It was a ridiculous thought, and yet . . . Damn, why couldn't happiness be as simple as holding onto the right moment and never letting it leave?

Sighing, he watched as she collected her riding boots and stockings and limped to a nearby tree stump. She sat down and dried her feet with her skirts, and then tugged her stockings over her damp skin.

"Here. Allow me." He arose and picked up her boot. He knelt on the one knee that didn't hurt and held out his hand. "Give me your foot."

"I can do it."

"Of course you can. But I'm being polite which, as you know, does not come easy to me, so do me a favor and give me your foot."

Humor warmed her eyes. "No gentleman has ever offered to assist me with my boots."

"I'm no gentleman, am I? I don't have to follow the rules." When she didn't lift her foot, he sighed. "Fine. You may consider this payment for the assistance I am about to demand of you."

"What assistance?" She couldn't have looked more suspicious.

"If you and that monster horse of yours don't lead me free of these trees, they will find my body in a few days, a thorn vine wrapped around my throat."

A reluctant chuckle bubbled from her. "Balesboro has been very cruel to you."

"So save me from this vile forest." He held her out his hand. "Your foot, please."

With a grin, she plopped her stockinged foot into his hand.

"Thank you." The feel of her damp skin through her stockings sent sparks up his arms and into other, more insistent parts. Ignoring it, he slipped the boot over her foot, tugging it firmly into place. He lowered her foot to the ground and picked up her other boot. "Now the other one."

She was less hesitant this time, so he lingered, admiring the roundness of her calf and the perfect turn of her ankle. There was something about this auburn-haired waif that piqued his senses, and he had yet to figure out what it was. He finished settling her boot in place and rocked back on his heels. "There."

"Thank you." She stood, collected her hat, and then went to collect Angelica. "We can both ride, if you'd like."

He followed her to the horse. "This beast would bolt if I ever dared throw a leg over her. I'll help you up, and then I'll stay nearby, if she'll let me. Come." He bent down and cupped his hands, ready to boost Charlotte into the saddle. "Up you go."

She held her riding skirts to one side and placed a hand on his shoulder, ready to settle her foot into his hands.

But he had other, better plans. When she was close enough, he straightened, grasped her by the waist, and lifted her into the saddle.

She clutched at his shoulder to steady herself, blushing as she did so. But she didn't pull away and even mumbled, "Thank you." Her horse, who'd been watching, turned her head back toward the trail as if satisfied all was as it should be.

Charlotte slanted a glance at the sun and grimaced. "We need to go. My aunt will be waiting."

"Of course." And yet Marco stayed where he was, looking up at her, his hands on her waist, a thousand thoughts racing through his mind. In less than two weeks, he would finish the commission. Two short weeks. *It isn't enough, damn it. I want so much more.*

So apparently, did she, for her gaze met his, her eyes dark under the brim of her hat. To his astonishment, she slid a hand over his where it rested at her waist. "I've been reading more of that book I told you about."

He tried not to focus on the way her fingers were entwined with his. *What did she just say?* "The book. The one about sculpting."

She nodded. "I would like to see some of your techniques as you make the fireplace surround." She wet her lips as if they were dry. "I am quite curious about your process."

"You are always welcome in my workshop. I will try to answer any questions you may have." He squeezed her hand once, and then stepped back, as happy as an angel just granted his wings.

She looked pleased and adorably self-conscious. "Thank you. I look forward to it."

"So do I." He took the reins, making sure he left plenty of loose leather between him and Angelica on the off chance she decided to nip at him. Satisfied she wasn't already eyeing him like a large apple, he glanced back at Charlotte and smiled. "Which way do we go?"

CHAPTER 10

Marco returned to his workshop to find Pietro sweeping the floors. The stonemason, unaware that Marco had just spent an enjoyable hour with the woman he shouldn't have spent an enjoyable hour with, didn't notice that his master was in a better than normal mood.

But he was. A much better mood, and all because of a beautiful, secret grotto in the heart of Balesboro Wood and a refreshingly candid woman with a soul as beautiful as her blue eyes.

That was why he felt like whistling as he found his chisel and hammer and set to work. Naturally, none of his cheerfulness had to do with the fact Charlotte was no longer marrying–

Marco squinted at the ceiling. *What was that man's name again?*

He shrugged. *Oh well. No matter. He is gone.* Satisfied, Marco angled the chisel and tapped it lightly, a chip flicking off the statue and falling to the floor.

Pietro put away his broom and came to watch Marco work. The stonemason grunted his approval. "It goes well."

Marco, who'd been chipping the stone away from a dimpled elbow, sat back on his heels. "There are two types of statue. One of them will fight you as you try to draw it from the stone. There are chips and broken rock, hard spots that cannot be smoothed, and smooth spots that cannot be carved. The stone and the statue struggle against one another, and the artist is caught between."

"I know those well. What is the other kind?"

"The statue is strong, and the stone knows it is beaten before the fight begins, so it steps aside. It allows the statue to emerge unscathed. These pillars are the second type of statue. I can see the figures so clearly that to me, the rest of the stone is already dust."

"They will be some of your best work."

"They will be magnificent." He went back to work.

After a while, Pietro announced that he'd been invited by Davis and the other grooms to play cards, but would go only if Marco didn't need him.

"Go," Marco said. "I won't need you any more today. Just don't lose. I'll not have you returning to Italy as naked as the day you were born because you lost all of your possessions in a card game."

"I promise to cheat as hard as I can and to never wager my final pair of breeches," Pietro vowed solemnly.

"You are a man of great sense." Marco waved the servant away. "Go. Enjoy yourself."

Chuckling, the stonemason left, and Marco continued his work, carefully tapping away at the white marble.

It had been a good day. Of course, he was still angry at that damned owl. The sketch was still gone, and Marco's hands still scratched, his knee was still stiff, but as painful and humiliating as his foray into the woods had been, it had been worth it to spend an hour in a beautiful grotto with an intriguing and seductive woman.

She was all of that and more, he decided, fitting the chisel to the fold of the caryatid's inner elbow. He wondered if Charlotte's elbow was as dimpled. *She didn't seem the least remorseful that she'd ended her engagement, too.* He'd been relieved at that.

He paused, the hammer cocked, the chisel in place, and wondered why he cared. Even though Charlotte was no longer engaged, she was still the daughter of his patron, and when her mother discovered that her daughter was no longer engaged, plans would be made for another marriage. Another suitor would be found.

And if that didn't work out, then there would be another.

And another.

And ano—

He slammed the hammer onto the chisel head, a loud ring echoing. An awkwardly shaped chunk of marble fell to the floor with a thunk.

Cursing, he examined the spot he'd hit, and was relieved to find that although he'd removed more than he'd meant to, his error hadn't destroyed the statue's lines.

Good God, he had to be careful. Scowling, his earlier good mood destroyed, he dropped his tools on the ground and left them.

What is wrong with me? Of course, Charlotte will have other suitors. God knows she deserved a swarm of them. He knew that, and expected it. Marriage was the goal of all well born women. It was what they were raised to do.

The problem was that, as hard as he tried, he couldn't imagine a man worthy of her. She was kind, funny, fascinating, complicated, spirited, and—He closed his eyes. *And not for me.*

He could not seem to remember that when she was nearby.

He rubbed his face, gritted his teeth, reclaimed his dropped tools, and went back to work. *Damn all this thinking; I need to finish these. For the rest of the day, that's all I'm going to think about.*

Soon the tap tap tap of the hammer filled the room, and the chips flew. Dust clung to his clothing and skin. As the hours passed, his hands and shoulders ached with his efforts. It was difficult, but every time thoughts of Charlotte threatened to return, he would mercilessly tap the thought away, letting the chips drop into a pile at his feet.

Marco worked through dinner and into the night, pausing only when Pietro came staggering home, coins jingling in his pockets. The stonemason mumbled an incoherent story about a marked card that somehow ended up under his chair and fell as he tried to climb into his cot. The old man ended up on the floor, laughing hysterically, until – finally – with a hearty wheeze, he rolled onto his side and fell asleep. Marco stopped long enough to put a pillow under the old man's head before returning to work.

Hours later, Marco stepped back and examined the pillars, rolling his shoulders where they'd knotted. The features were now clear, the arms and legs almost done, as were the graceful folds of the toga. Tomorrow, he would leave the chisel and hammer behind, and start smoothing the stone.

His gaze flickered to the uncarved faces and he growled under his breath. *Soon, my muse, you must do your job and reveal them to me.*

His muse remained silent, and so – tired and aching – he went outside to the well to wash before he stumbled to his bed to sleep.

He awoke late the next morning to a soft rain thrumming on the roof. He sat up and stretched away the familiar stiffness of his arms and shoulders, wincing more at the ache in his heart than in his limbs. His time by the pool with Charlotte now felt like a too-beautiful dream. Yesterday, every tap of his hammer had driven home the sad realities of their situation and he couldn't shake the darkness it left. Sighing heavily, he put on clean breeches and a fresh shirt, tugged on his boots, and raked his hands through his hair. Stretching his arms over his head, he made his way to his workshop and found the fire freshly stoked, warding off the chill brought by the rain. On his work table sat a plate holding an apple, a wedge of cheese, and some bread. Pietro, however, was nowhere to be seen. *No wonder Simmons has decided he dislikes you, old friend. You have taken up permanent residence in the kitchens, and no one likes a distracted cook.*

Famished, Marco ate, his gaze wandering to the statues. While he waited for the muse to whisper, he would work on smoothing out the chisel lines. He would use a special rasp to knock of the larger lines made by the chisel. When that was done, he'd polish the stone until the surface was silky and shiny. Where should be begin, he wondered? On the arms, perhaps. They provided the most movement in both pieces. He pushed his empty plate aside and found his tools.

Working kept him from dwelling on the decision he'd made yesterday. Slowly, slowly, the rasp did its work and the chisel lines were erased, leaving only the sheen of milky white marble, ready for polishing. It was laborious, but the beauty of the end result pushed him onward.

Still, the blank faces irked him. He stopped working, closed his eyes, and tried to imagine them, but his stubborn muse remained silent.

Muttering, he set aside his tools and repaired to his work table. He found some foolscap and a stick of charcoal, and began to sketch, trying various shapes for the faces, different noses and lips, different curves for the cheek. Anything to tease the muse to life.

He'd just sketched a series of eyes when the stable door opened, the thrum of the rain loud. But instead of Pietro, Charlotte rushed inside, a blanket held over her bonneted head, water dripping from every surface.

"Goodness, it's coming down!" She threw off the blanket and tossed it over a barrel sitting near the door and brushed raindrops from her spencer. "It's raining hard. The drops are splashing on the ground like marbles tossed into a tea cup."

Marco nodded, and wondered why his workshop suddenly felt too small, too intimate. Truth be told, he was painfully glad to see her, but that same happiness was tinged with the cold whisper of his future despair. "It's too dark in here. I'll light some lamps." He collected three lamps from where they hung on hooks, and lit each one, turning them up as high as he dared before he returned them to their places. Soon the workshop was bathed in a soft glow.

The light reflected off of Charlotte's red spencer and the yellow gown the peeked beneath it. Despite the fact that her wet hem dragged the ground and mud had spattered over her half boots, she still looked like what she was – a beautiful young lady of the best birth, rich in heritage, and destined to carry on an ancient family name.

She untied her bonnet, pulled it off, and shook her curls free, the auburn color warm in the cool dampness of his workshop.

He shoved his hands in his pockets to keep from reaching for the few pins still holding her hair in place and letting down her tortured tresses.

"I hope I'm not disturbing your work." She placed her bonnet on his work table, making sure she didn't set it on any papers that might absorb the dampness. "I was out taking a walk and it began to sprinkle, so I was forced to take refuge here."

"It's been raining for hours. And where did you get this blanket? Did you find it on your walk?"

Her lips quivered. "Don't be ridiculous. I got the blanket from an old witch in exchange for an apple I was carrying in my pocket."

Damn it, why did she have to make him laugh? It made it impossible to stay cross, and he needed his irritation. "Fortunately for you," he said in a pointed tone, "it is a short distance to the Hall. You should leave now, before the rain gets worse."

She sent him a searching look, and he could see that she was surprised at his coolness. Her eyes narrowed, but all she said was, "I brought you something." She pulled a slender tome from her pocket and held it out. "It's the book on sculpting I found in the library."

"Thank you." He took it, almost wincing when her fingers brushed his. Turning, he placed it on his folio where it rested on the desk. "You'd better go now. The sky's getting darker."

Her jaw firmed. "No."

His heart sank. She wasn't going to make this easy.

"I think I'll stay here until the rain lets up." She crossed to the stove and held her hands toward the fire. Overhead the rain thrummed on the roof. Before she'd come in, his workshop had felt damp and dim. Now, it seemed cozy and incredibly warm. Perhaps lighting the lamps hadn't been such a good idea.

She glanced at him from under her lashes, and proffered a smile. "I love rainy weather, don't you?"

God, but he would miss that smile. He would miss the way she smelled, of lily and sunshine, and the way she peeped at him from under her lashes when she thought he wasn't looking – He would miss all of it, all of her.

But that didn't change the facts of their lives. "Charlotte, I know how we left things yesterday, but . . . we can't do this."

Her smile froze in place. "Do what?"

But she already knew. He could see it in her eyes, in the faint quiver of her bottom lip. He forced himself to continue. "Our time in the woods was perfect, and I didn't want it to end. Being there with you . . . it felt as if we could overcome anything. As if we were meant to be."

Her smile had faded, her eyes darkening. "Perhaps we are."

"Are we? To what end? To the detriment of our families? Yours would be horrified at this connection and mine would suffer from my loss of career – Could our love bear that weight?" He shook his head. "We can't take that chance. Too many would suffer. We must be prudent and—"

"No!" She took a step toward him. "I don't want to do the safe thing, the 'right' thing, especially when that 'right' thing is defined by others. I've tried that, and it was the most deadening thing I've ever done. This attraction, this passion, whatever we have, it's real. You know it and I know it. It's meant to be. If we walk away from this chance, how do we know we'll have another? Marco, we should at least try."

"To what end? Every day we spend together will make the inevitable all the more difficult." He was worried; he was worried about how enraptured he was already. He worried about how much more enthralled he'd be if he continued to see her. He was worried about how painful it would be to leave her behind and how empty his life would be after that.

But most of all, he worried about how she would survive the weight of another loss. She'd suffered enough. He sent her a bleary look. "I can't do this." *Not to you. Not after all you've already been there.*

She tucked a stray curl behind her ear, her eyes bright with unshed tears. "This is so unfair." She gave a weak laugh. "When I came today, I was hoping for something else."

"So was I, but we must be realistic."

She didn't look at all happy with that. "What if we keep our conversation centralized on safe topics like the weather or—or cats, or something."

"Cats?" He had to smile, although it killed him. "It wouldn't matter if we didn't talk at all. Every minute I spend with you will haunt me more. Go back to Nimway. I can't—"

"No! Not yet. I want to stay. At least for a while." She looked around, her movement abrupt, desperate. "There! You've been working on the pillars." She crossed to them before he could stop her.

Damn it, I should have covered those blasted things.

She stood before them, her eyes moving over every inch of the statues. "Oh Marco," she said in a soft voice. "They're perfect."

Warmth washed over him at her admiration. He wanted to stand beside her and explain all he'd done, but he forced himself to stay in place, far away where he was safer. "The muse has hidden the faces, but I'll see them soon."

She nodded. "I'd heard you'd been hard at work on these, but I had no idea you were this close to finishing."

"Who told you I'd been hard at work?"

"Pietro told Cook, who told Simmons, who told me, but not before he'd complained about the amount of time Pietro has spent in the kitchens and how Simmons is certain the missing ham is now residing in Pietro's rather large belly." She frowned. "There was also something about pickled eggs, although I didn't catch all of it."

"Good God. I'm going to skin Pietro alive."

"Not if Simmons gets to him first." She bent and picked up a marble chip and turned it over in her hands, smoothing it as she did so. "To think that something so beautiful came from a plain block of stone. It gives one hope, doesn't it?"

He tried not to watch her, but he couldn't help himself. Her hands were as beautiful as the rest of her, slender and narrow, and as graceful as the fall of water over a smooth rock.

Absently, he reached for his charcoal and paper, his fingers itching to capture her expression as she examined the marble. He wouldn't render her as the daughter of a wealthy scion, a maid of virtue and the utmost respectability as her blood demanded. No, he'd follow instead the wildness of her deep blue gaze, the sensual line of her mouth contrasted with the carefully protected life she'd led. He would capture the fullness of her breasts, and the delicate hollows of her shoulders, both of which begged to be explored and tasted. He would have her reclined on a chaise, nude except for a silk shawl, which he'd drape over her bared thighs—

Snap. The charcoal stick broke between his fingers. He stared down at the splintered ruin, his mind still spinning.

The marble chips clattered as she returned them to the pile. "The pillars are quite tall. Almost my height."

"Almost." Marco tossed the broken charcoal onto the table.

"The fireplace is to be the focal point for the room, so those had to be substantial."

"That will be is a lot of marble."

"It's a big fireplace."

Her lips twitched. "True." She turned from the pillars and walked toward him, her gaze flickering past him to his work table. "So many sketches! What were you working on when I came in?"

He stepped between her and the table, even though it put him far too close to her for his comfort. "Charlotte . . . please. This is only making it harder."

"Good." She smiled up at him, and he was surprised to see flecks of gold in her blue eyes, reflected from the gray, rainy light. "If I'm to be forgotten, I don't want it to be done easily."

Overhead, the rain thrummed, while the scent of lily filled the space between them. He rammed his hands back into his pockets. "The rain is getting harder. If you want to reach Nimway without getting soaked, you should—"

She darted around him, grabbed a handful of sketches, and dashed away before he could do more than curse.

He yanked his hands from his pockets and stalked after her, but she sprinted around a pole in the center of the room, her skirts fluttering as she whisked herself to the farthest corner where she stopped near a lamp and looked at the pages she'd stolen.

"Give those back!"

"No." Her gaze devoured the pages as she turned through them. "They're wonderfully done."

He lunged for them, but she spun out of reach, dashing to the other side of the workshop without taking her eyes off his drawings.

"You're going to trip and fall."

"You'll catch me." She didn't even look up as she said it.

He scowled, even as he acknowledged she was right. If she fell, he would catch her. *Every time, for as long as I'm able.*

She reached the final page. "I had no idea you could draw as well as this."

"They're not well drawn when your father is a world-famous painter."

"I can't imagine he'd have anything negative to say about these. They're so vivid." She held up the sketches he'd made of several different types of mouths. "I never knew there were so many types of lips, and they're all drawn so realistically."

He tried to drag his attention from her mouth and failed. There may be a hundred different types of lips, but only one set beckoned him, tormented him, bewitched him.

She lowered the pages. "You're trying to design the faces for your pillars."

He held out his hand. "I'll take those."

She made a face but brought him the pages.

He took them and then, to put a safe distance between them, he turned on his heel and carried them back to his work table.

To his chagrin, she followed, stopping just short of him, her gaze locked with his.

He cursed under his breath, wanting her so badly that he burned with it. "You are killing me."

"Good." She frowned. "I thought I overthought things. That is one of my flaws. But you . . . you are much better at it than I could ever be. Marco, don't do this. We should take what happiness we can. And if, at the end of your time here, we decide the cost is too high, then we'll deal with it then."

"That will only entangle us further, and you know it."

"So?"

"So the pain will be that much more. Charlotte, what if that short span of time costs us the happiness of the rest of our lives? Every time I see you, it's not enough. I think about you constantly when I'm awake, and you visit my dreams when I'm asleep. I'm already aching with wanting you, and aching at the thought of leaving you. I don't know if this is love or passion, or if it will last to the end of the month, or carry us forever." He spread his hands wide. "All I know is that seeing you more and then leaving you will cut my soul until it begs for release."

She'd paled as he spoke, and now she whispered, "I feel the same way. It's horrible and wonderful at the same time."

"Which is why we should end this now, before it's too late."

She looked at him, her eyes suspiciously bright. After a long moment, she whispered, "If that's how you feel, then there's nothing more for me to say."

His throat ached with tightness, but he nodded.

"Fine." Her movements tight, she swept past him and grabbed her bonnet and slapped it on her head, the ribbons trailing over her shoulders.

She started for the door, but then spun to face him. "But I'm going to say one thing first. You told me that your father spent all that time painting portraits of people who were rich with gold and poor with happiness. You are consigning us to that same fate, a life of unhappiness. I don't deserve that, and neither do you. And don't say we have responsibilities to our families, for I'm well aware of it. But if our families cannot accept us finding our happiness, then our efforts need to be directed toward helping them to do so, not in abandoning what we've found."

God, was she right? "Charlotte, have we found happiness? Or is it just a temporary fascination? What if we act on this and then, months from now, we realize we've made an error?"

Her eyes flashed, and she lifted her chin until she looked like a mighty goddess ready to toss a thunderbolt. "If you don't know what you want, and you don't believe we are worth fighting for, then there's nothing more I can say." She picked up the damp blanket and opened the door, the downpour roaring.

He watched her, the lump in his throat growing until he couldn't breathe. His heart begged him to stop her, to say something and say it quickly, while his head reminded him of the icy realities of the choice they faced, of the life he'd be condemning both her and his family to if he stole her away. No love could survive that.

Not even this one.

Lightning flashed, followed by a boom of thunder that made the ground tremble. Rain roared down.

"Wait." He took a step forward. "The lightning is close. Stay here until—"

She whisked her blanket over her head and plunged into the rain, the empty doorway standing open behind her.

CHAPTER 11

Charlotte crossed her arms behind her head and stared up at the blue sky, the hum of bees melding with the scent of sun-warmed grass. This, she decided, just might be her favorite place in the world. She was stretched out on her back in the field near the lake, hidden away by a wall of golden grasses. She'd made a bed for herself by walking in a circle until the grass had flattened. Then, for comfort and to keep the still-damp ground from seeping into her gown, she'd thrown her cloak over the crushed stalks. Now she had a secret, cozy nest with nothing but blue sky overhead.

When she'd been younger, she used to make these nests all of the time. But it had been years since she'd bothered. She crossed her bared feet at the ankles and brushed away an errant ant trying to climb up her sleeve.

It was lovely today, and warm, and so long as she didn't think about Marco or Caroline or the sudden dreariness of life in general, she could hold the tears at bay. She had better things to do than think about those things, anyway.

She plucked a stalk of grass and ran it through her finger, the prickly seeds scattering, drops of gold that glistened in the sun as they fell. Some grains disappeared on the ground, while others clung to her skirts like so many seed pearls. It was nice to be alone, truly alone, with no dark, disturbing eyes watching her and making her feel things she shouldn't.

Yesterday, for the first time since Caroline's death, as Charlotte had dashed through the rain to visit Marco, she'd been happy. But he'd cut her euphoria short in the cruelest of ways. "Scoundrel," she muttered, reaching out to yank another long blade of grass from the stalks around her.

She supposed it was flattering that he feared he'd already come to care for her too much. It softened her wounded pride a little, although the comfort was scant. "Bloody fool!" she announced, startling a beetle that had been crawling on the grass near her head to swoop up into the air and fly away.

Scowling, she plucked two more stalks and braided them together. *What would I be doing about this horrid situation if Caroline were still alive? Would I be here, in the grass, plaiting grass? Or would I be in Marco's workshop, making it very hard for him not to fall in love with me?*

Charlotte knew the answer and was certain Caroline would approve. Much to Mama's chagrin, Caroline had grown starry-eyed every time a maid from Nimway had fallen in love with a footman. When she could, Caroline had taken great pleasure in assisting those romances, passing notes and finding ways to get the lovebirds together without Simmons being any the wiser.

Charlotte tossed the plaited grass blades away and crossed her arms back under her head, wondering why she'd allowed Marco to talk so much. *I could have changed his mind with a kiss, I know I could have. Why didn't I think of that?* It was a sad fact of life that one often thought of the perfect reaction to a situation well after it was over.

The next time she saw Marco, she would let him know that while she appreciated his candor, she wasn't going to disappear into thin air. She wasn't a meek and mild miss, not any more.

Caroline would approve of that, too, Charlotte realized with a smile. Caroline had always said that Charlotte's happiness would never be encased in silks and satins. No, her happiness lay in the stream of sunshine spilling over her face, the feel of grass beneath her bare toes. And now her happiness lay in the deep brown eyes of a forbidden man.

"But why must he be so *bossy?*" Charlotte asked a butterfly as it flittered softly overhead. The comforting buzz of bees and the mesmerizing sway of the grass soothed her irritation, as the warm sun made her eyes heavy.

She was so sleepy. She let her eyes flutter shut, just for a moment . . .

She awoke to the sound of dripping water.

Confused, she looked around her and her memory came flooding back. Ah yes, she was still in her nest. She sat up, shading her eyes as she glanced up at the sun. It was much later than she'd expected.

The slow drip that had awakened her became a splash. *What is that?*

She rose up on her knees and peered through the grass toward the lake – and there he was. Marco was waist deep in the blue water. He'd chosen a corner far from Nimway, hidden from the house behind a screen of trees, but entirely too visible from where she sat. Bold, beautiful, and as naked as the day he was born, he washed his chest with a cake of soap, the sun glistening off his wet shoulders as suds slid down his broad, defined chest.

Charlotte blinked, unable to look away and unwilling to move, she stayed where she was.

He lifted the wet cloth over his head and squeezed it, water streaming onto his head and down his face. He had such a fascinating face, all hard planes and straight lines. His jaw was as marked as they came, his nose bold, his mouth hard. She wondered what it would be like to be in the lake with him, to feel at the same time, the coolness of the water and the heat of his skin.

She bit her lip. She'd wager ten guineas that even in cold water, his skin would be warm – searing, even. She parted the golden grasses for a better view, admiring the muscles of his shoulders and arms, the dark hair that traced over his broad chest and then thinned into a line that lead down his stomach to disappear into the water. She lifted up on her heels, trying to see—

"Miss Charlotte! Hello?" Simmons called from the direction of the Hall.

Charlotte dropped lower in the grass.

His voice came closer, alternating between shouting her name and speaking to someone who seemed to be following him. Charlotte glanced up at the sky and winced. The modiste had arrived and now the search was on.

Charlotte peered through the and caught sight of the butler as he marched down the path toward the lake, Aunt Verity scurried behind, her face flushed as she fanned herself with a lace handkerchief.

"This is a travesty!" Aunt Verity said in a waspish tone. "She's been gone for hours. Was no one worried about the poor thing?"

"We worry about her all of the time! But as you know, it is Miss Charlotte's way to disappear for hours on end."

"On a horse! The groom said Angelica hasn't been ridden today."

"We didn't know that, did we?" he snapped back. After a moment, he said in a tightly controlled tone, "I'm certain we'll find her at the lake. She used to come here often, and most likely still does."

Oh no! They are going to the lake and Marco is— She turned to peer back at the lake and was relieved to find him gone. The only evidence he'd been there was the trace of bubbles floating on the water as it lapped gently against the bank.

Was he even now heading toward the stables? She lifted higher on her knees, ready to drop back into the grass if Simmons or Aunt Verity turned her way. Perhaps he'd gone by—

A strong arm wrapped about her waist and pulled her to the ground. She was now on her back, held against a large, warm, damp body as she stared up at a head outlined by sunlight. "Mar—"

He placed a finger over her lips. "Shh!"

And indeed, she could hear Aunt Verity's drawling tones much closer now, asking why on earth Simmons had thought to find Charlotte in such an untamed, damp place as a lake.

Marco kept his finger against her lips as he bent close to whisper, "We must be quiet. They will leave soon."

Charlotte nodded, noting that he'd managed to put on his breeches, but not his shirt and his bared skin rested against her arm. She grasped his wrist and tugged his hand from her mouth. "You knew I was here," she whispered.

Reluctant amusement warmed his eyes. "You are not a very good spy." His warm breath tickled her ear.

"I wasn't spying," she whispered back, irked because he was partially right. "I was here first. I fell asleep and when I woke up, there you were."

He didn't look as if he believed her, but wisely, he didn't say so.

Nearby, Aunt Verity was still chastising Simmons, but having found no evidence of Charlotte at the lake, they ever already heading back to the Hall.

Charlotte and Marco waited. She'd been right about his skin. Even fresh from the cold lake, he was as warm as the sun. His bare chest pressed against her arm, and she had to fight the desire to turn toward him. *He would push you away. He's already decided how this relationship will end.*

She frowned. She was tired of Marco deciding everything for them as if he were the only one capable of decisions. It was time she made some decisions of her own. They might only have a week and a half left, but if she had her way, it would be the best week and a half they'd ever had. And if, at the end of that time, they were forced to end it . . . No. She refused to bow to a mere threat of impending sadness. By God, she was a Harrington, and Harringtons never flinched.

She found herself smiling. It felt so good to be herself again, to push against the norms and the expectations and the rules that tried to hem one into place. And with that return to the old Charlotte, came the familiar urge to break every code of behavior society forced upon her. To laugh louder, dance faster, and talk more than was permitted.

A door closed at the Hall, and she could no longer hear either Aunt Verity or the butler.

"There."

Marco started to get up, but she was quicker. She slipped her arms around his neck and held him there. "You invaded my fort, so now you must pay the price."

He blinked down at her, his brows drawn. "Charlotte, don't—"

"Don't tell me what to do. Pay the price or else."

He thought about standing and walking away, she saw it in his eyes, so she rolled toward him, pressing her chest to his.

His gaze darkened. "What's your price?"

Ah, sweet success. She smiled. "A kiss. Two, if you don't do it properly the first time."

"I . . ." He pressed his mouth into a firm line. "No. I can't." He tugged her arms from his neck. Freed, he sat upright and started to stand.

"Wait!" She sat up, too, and yanked at the lacings of her gown, undoing them so fast her hands blurred.

"Charlotte," he hissed. "What are you doing?"

"You can see what I'm doing. I'm untying my gown."

"Why?" He had the same look in his eyes as the deer she sometimes startled when riding through Balesboro.

She tugged her gown free, pulling out one arm, and then the

other, shivering more from her boldness than anything else. "You bathed naked in the lake. Now it's my turn."

"You can't do that."

"Why not?"

"It wouldn't be safe. Someone might see you and—" He clamped his mouth closed, looking adorably mulish. "I won't allow it."

"I either want to bathe in the lake, or I want a kiss." She pushed her gown to her hips and then stood. The heavy skirts fell to her ankles. She kicked them to one side and then unlaced her underskirts. They quickly joined her gown, leaving her wearing nothing but her thin, lace chemise.

Marco groaned. "You can't do this."

"Watch me." Chilly from the breeze, she reached for the tie at her neck.

"You won't do it," he said desperately, as if his harsh tone would make it happen. "No well brought up young lady would ever—"

Her chemise fell to her feet, the fine lawn ruffling in the breeze.

With a muffled curse, Marco grabbed her and swung her back to the ground, his warm body covering hers. His face was dark with fury. "What are you doing?"

"This." She slipped her arms back around his neck and kissed him. She didn't kiss him gently, but with the blazing passion that even now flooded through her. God, but she'd wanted this, needed it even.

Marco moaned once and then, lost forever, he followed her into her sweet madness. His hands moved over her, cupping her breasts, sliding down her stomach and then back. His bared skin against hers felt deliciously decadent and she urged him on, following instincts as old as time, seducing him even as she was seduced.

For the life of him, Marco couldn't remember a word of their last conversation. Right now, all he could think about was how sweet she tasted, how her breasts filled his hands when he cupped them, how the silk of her skin drove him mad. She was as succulent and honeyed as a ripe pear, and he was determined to taste her.

She ran her hands over his chest, each stroke driving him mad. He moved a hand to his breeches and, without breaking the kiss, loosened the button and shoved them off. Now he felt all of her, naked and writhing, and damned it if it still wasn't enough.

Charlotte reveled in the rough skin of his hands, in the wildness of his kisses. His tongue met hers, and she answered him with such fervor that he moaned against her. She had no fear, a slave to her own wild, heated passion. Her thighs grew slick with her desire, and she moved restlessly, pressing her hips to him.

He broke the kiss and lifted up on his elbow, panting heavily. His eyes had never been so dark, his expression so intense. "Roll over," he whispered.

"What?"

A wicked smile touched his lips.

Trepidation flickered through her, as heady as their passion. God, but she loved the uncertainty of life, of love, of this man. She rolled to her stomach, and he pushed her hair to one side and kissed her shoulder. She shivered as he slid his kiss to her neck. With one kiss after another, he made his way down her back, to the rounded cheek of her ass, murmuring her name, and telling her in bold detail all of the things he wanted to do to her. He told her the ways he would take her, and how many times he would make her cry his name. Each kiss was both torment and tease. And she was possessed, fully and completely, her body heating as, aching with need, she writhed under his ministrations.

He stopped and lifted up on his arm. Desperate with want, she started to turn over, but he imprisoned her against him, his hand warm over her breast, her back against his chest, his cock hard against her. "Do you feel this, my love?" he whispered, his voice more growl than else. He ran his hand over the curve of her hip and slipped his hand between her thighs. He stroked her, showing her what madness pleasure could be.

She gasped, but he didn't stop, the roughness of his calloused fingers never still. He stroked, insistent and firm as she arched wildly against him. It was such an intimate touch, and heated longing grew inside her.

He must have sensed she was ready, for just as she gasped his name, he flipped her onto her back, positioned himself between her thighs, and took her with a rough passion. She answered in kind, her legs wrapped around his hips, one hand clutched in his thick hair, the other splayed on his lower back as she met him, thrust for thrust. Somewhere in the madness, there was a faint pain, but it was obscured when, shocking and thorough, waves of pleasure wracked her.

Oh God, nothing had ever felt so good. She clung to him, unable to think, struggling to breathe as he buried his face in her neck, gasping her name as he collapsed beside her, as spent as she.

For the longest time, they remained where they were, entwined and breathless. Charlotte soaked in the feel of him, aware of every sensation, every feeling. She savored the weight of his shoulder where it rested against hers, the warmth of his skin, the stickiness of her thighs, the sweetness of his breath where it brushed her bared neck. *I could stay here forever and never want for another thing.*

But that wasn't true of course, and to her chagrin, her stomach rumbled.

Marco lifted his head. "You, my lady, have worked up an appetite."

She opened one eye. "A gentleman would have ignored that."

He laughed and moved against her, his thigh rubbing hers as he buried his face against her neck to murmur, "What more must I do to convince you that I'm no gentleman?"

She slipped her arms around his neck. "I'm sure you'll think of something."

"Oh, I will." He pulled her closer. They stayed there, the sun warming their bared skin. He rested his head on her shoulder and ran his hand lightly over her stomach and then up to her breast. Back and forth he trailed his fingers, stirring her body back to life.

This time, she ignored the trembling. As much as she hated to destroy this perfect moment, there were things that must be dealt with. She took a steady breath, and then said quietly, "This changes everything."

His hands stilled. He was silent for a long time. "It cannot."

"But it has."

He lifted up on his elbow, his brows knit. "Charlotte, we—"

"Yes. We. Not you, making decisions for us. But us, making decisions for us. That's what a 'we' is."

He frowned. "I was doing what was best for us."

"No, you were doing what you *thought* was best for us. There is no one answer to life. Caroline's death taught me that."

His gaze never left her face. "What do you suggest?"

"We are still discovering things about one another."

"That's an optimistic way to say we don't know one another well enough."

"I've been told by an expert that if two people are in love, that even if they were to live together a thousand years, they would still be learning things about one another."

He dropped his forehead to hers. "God, but I want to believe you."

"Then do. Take a chance on us, Marco. I'm willing to."

He shook his head. "You would never be happy if your family broke with you. I don't want to be the cause of that."

"Then we'll have to see to it that they don't overreact. That they come to see you as I do."

"Your mother may not see it as 'overreacting.'"

Charlotte smiled. "Perhaps we've given her too little credit.

But it doesn't matter, this is a chance I must take. A chance *we* must take together."

He looked as if he wanted to believe her so badly, and yet was afraid of doing so. "You make it seem so simple."

"Maybe it is. Maybe we're the ones who've made it difficult. And maybe . . . maybe it doesn't matter."

She watched as he thought through her words.

Into this quiet, he surprised her with a chuckle.

"What?"

"You said you didn't have the mark of Nimway."

She looked at him. "I don't."

His smile faded. "But . . . you do. I saw it. It's on your shoulder right where—

She sat up, straining to look.

And there it was. An oval mark, paler than Caroline's had been, to be sure, but an oval just the same. Shocked, she looked at Marco. "I'm the guardian."

"Apparently so." He pulled her back into his arms. "You didn't know."

"I never saw it. It . . . it didn't used to be there."

"Well, now it is. Perhaps the sun brought it out like a freckle." He tucked her against him and rested his cheek against her hair.

"Perhaps," she said, although she didn't believe it. She was the guardian. What did that mean, she wondered. *What if . . . what if it means whatever I want?*

For some reason, the thought made her smile. She wasn't the only one with the mark; Mama had it, too, just like Caroline.

Marco pressed a kiss to her forehead. "You are right. Perhaps I was hasty in assigning us to failure."

"Oh, you were hasty. You very hasty."

He chuckled. "Then let me show you how unhasty I can be." He bent to kiss a trail from her neck to her shoulder and lower, sending shivers through her yet again.

CHAPTER 12

Marco stepped back from the pillars and ran his fingers over the smooth, polished stone. He was almost done. It was late, but he'd been too restless to sleep, his thoughts churning over his time with Charlotte. Because he was so invigorated, he'd used the wild energy on his work. He'd sanded and shaped, chiseled and polished, even as he thought about her, her words, the shape of her breasts – every delicious detail. Letting his mind wander had awoken his muse and to his deep satisfaction, the faces had appeared under the tip of his chisel without the use of a single sketch.

Pietro came inside, yawning widely. "You're still up! Did you see the basket of potato cakes from Cook?"

"I did. That was very kind of her. I'd ask you to relay my thanks, but I'm sure you already have."

Pietro grinned. "I have indeed. I—" His gaze fell on the statues. "You're almost finished."

"I am."

Pietro slowly walked around the statues, squinting at the graceful lines of a toga. "good. Very good. Once the Queen sees this, she will want you to make fifteen new fireplaces for her palaces."

Marco traced his finger over a marble-smooth shoulder. "Sadly, that will not happen."

The stonemason cocked a shaggy brow. "What?"

"Suppose there was no reference to the Queen. No commission. No anything."

"Why would that happen? You've done a magnificent job with this work. There's no reason why Mrs. Harrington wouldn't recom—" The old man's face froze. "You didn't."

Marco tried not to look guilty. And indeed, he didn't feel guilty, but he wondered if he should. "I have decided to make my way without Mrs. Harrington's recommendation."

"It's more than that. What will you do when she tells the world you're not to be trusted with their daughters!" Pietro cursed heavily. "I knew this would happen. The way you two looked at each other, it was only a matter of time. You're just like your father, always dreaming about tomorrow and not doing enough for today."

"My father was happy when he was with my mother," Marco said sharply. "It's all he wanted. And I've realized that's all I want, too."

"And what of your family?"

"My brothers and sisters are no longer children. I keep thinking they are because I've been taking care of them for so long, but just look at them. They are already making their own way in the world, and could have been doing so much sooner had I let them. Besides, I know that they'll want me to be happy, too. It's what I would want for them."

"It will make things harder for them and you and everyone," the stonemason warned.

"I know."

"You might never make a decent commission again."

"Then I will deal with it." No, he and Charlotte would deal

with it, together.

Pietro threw up his hands. "You di Rossis, always spouting about true love. I will never understand it."

Marco chuckled.

The stonemason rubbed his neck. After a long while, he sighed. "I suppose there's nothing more to be said. It won't be easy, but you're right; it isn't the end of the world, either."

"Exactly. I can work in other countries, where I'm not yet known, and build my reputation there. Charlotte would enjoy traveling, and—"

Pietro threw up his hand. "I don't need to know all of your thoughts on the subject!"

"I'm sorry. I'm just happy."

"I suppose that's good," the old man said grudgingly. He looked at the statues for a long minute and then sighed. "You know what I think?"

"What?"

"I think you should do what you must. And wherever you go, I'll be glad to join you."

"Thank you," Marco said, touched by the stonemason's dedication.

Pietro, his face suspiciously red, jerked his head toward the statues. "Now finish those, will you? If we have to make a quick getaway, it would be better not to have to haul slabs of stone with us."

"We should be able to install it tomorrow."

"Good. I'll let Cook know I'm not long for her world. She will be truly sorry to see me go and will most likely ask me to spend the night. She has a nice bed, she does. And lots of pillows." Pietro ambled toward the door. As he did so, he cast a final glance at the pillars, and then stopped.

A smile split his face, the like of which Marco had never seen. "Your figures have changed since you first designed them."

Marco glanced absently at the pillars. "What's changed?"

"Everything. You've made them more—" The old man held his hands in front of his chest. "—bigger."

"You're crazed. This is exactly how I sketched them."

A noise that sounded suspiciously like a snort broke from the stonemason. He slapped a hand over his mouth and pretended to cough. As soon as he could speak, he blurted out, "Until later, then." He ducked out the door and hurried away.

Marco could hear the man's laughter all the way across the stable yard. *What in the hell is that about?* He examined the statues. Was Pietro right? Marco was sure he'd envisioned them this way from the beginning. He never veered once the muse arrived. *That fool doesn't remember what I sketched.*

Scowling, Marco went to his workbench and found his folio. He found his original sketches and glanced through them. As he did so, his eyes widened. *Good God. He's right.* The sketches showed two graceful poses of the same woman, as did his carving, but there the similarities ended. The goddess in his sketches was slender and winsome, fairylike in contour, while the goddess he'd carved was curvaceous, her hips and breasts full, her thighs more rounded, more like—

He lowered the sketches and turned back to the pillars, examining the face he'd carved just this evening. He dropped the papers onto his work table, unaware that half of them fell to the floor. *I couldn't have, not without knowing . . .* But he had. He knew that curvaceous, seductive body because he'd touched it. Knew that neck because he'd kissed it. Without thinking, he'd carved each figure with one leg slightly bent, which hid the curve of her back. He knew every inch of this goddess from the delicate feet, to the bold nose, to the curls that clustered about her delicate neck.

He rubbed his eyes, and then looked again, wondering if he was imagining things.

But he wasn't.

Suddenly, he was laughing as hard as Pietro. "Oh Charlotte, what have I done?"

CHAPTER 13

The light would not go away.

Charlotte, pulled from a deep dream where she and Marco were sailing away in a lovely ship on a sparkling still sea, fought waking up as if her life depended upon it. She didn't want to wake up, she wanted to stay on the ship with Marco and—

The light pulsed, and she threw up her hand to shield her eyes from the annoying lantern glow. Muttering to herself, she peeked through her fingers, ready to banish whoever was holding the bloody thing to the devil. But it wasn't a lantern at all. Instead, the mace head sat in her window, the moonstone reflecting the full moon that filled the night sky.

She'd never seen it burn so brightly. Rubbing her eyes, she threw her feet over the edge of the bed and went to where it sat, astonished at the brightness. Who in the world had put this here? She'd have a word with Simmons in the morning. It was too late now, for the house was silent, everyone asleep.

It had been a lovely day. Marco and his servant had spent most of it in the dining hall installing the new surround, hidden behind a wall of tarps that they'd hung over tall chairs to block their work from view. Despite Simmons's sharp stare and Aunt Verity's presence, Caroline had managed to sneak in to see Marco on more than one occasion. His servant had been faintly irked by her visits, but Marco had laughed and had even stolen a very passionate kiss.

He'd been playful, and she'd loved it, even when he'd refused to let her see the fireplace until it was finished. She hadn't pressed him; she'd seen his work as it had progressed, and had a very good idea of how it would look, anyway.

She set the mace head on her dresser where it couldn't channel the moonlight, and then turned to go back to bed. But as she passed by the window, something outside caught her eye.

Another light, this one small, almost tiny.

Unlike the moonstone, this light didn't sit quietly, but swooped and hopped, and then twinkled as it danced across the lawn.

Bewitched, Charlotte leaned closer to the window, her breath fogging the glass as she watched the light flicker in and out of sight, moving toward the woods. *That's the oddest thing. If it wasn't so cold outside, I would go and see –*

The light swooped toward the woods where a bridal path disappeared beside an old oak. With a final shimmer, it disappeared from sight.

Charlotte stared at the path, her mind suddenly racing.

It was night time.

A strange light had beckoned her into the wood.

Is this what sent Caroline into Balesboro in the middle of the night?

Charlotte's heart thudded against her collarbone. This had to be it. She reached back and touched the mark on her shoulder, the spot oddly warm under her fingers. She was the guardian now. If anyone was responsible for following mysterious lights, it was her.

She whirled from the window and hurried to her wardrobe. Moments later, she was dressed, her cloak hanging from her shoulders as she tip-toed downstairs. She needed a lamp and knew that two sat on a long marble table just outside the dining room. They were ornate affairs, but would cast a bright beam, which she'd need in the dark woods.

She made her way across the great hall, her boots muffled by the rugs, and reached the table holding the lamps. She picked up the closest and found a tinder box resting behind it. She lit the lamp and adjusted it to nice glow. She'd just turned to leave when her gaze fell on the open door to the dining hall. *Ah, yes, the fireplace.*

She didn't know what impulse held her, but to her surprise she found herself walking into the dining room, her lamp held aloft. The light flickered over the fireplace, the artwork drawing the eye as surely as a moth flew toward a flame. She drew closer, admiring the impressive work. It was a thing of beauty, the marble she'd watched chipped into submission. The crenelated mantle sat boldly over the carved header, the rope-twined decoration of the trim panels framing each side. Beyond them were the pillars Marco had struggled with, and had finally bested. Each depicted an almost naked beauty almost Charlotte's height. Their skin glowed alabaster white as they held the mantle over their heads, their breasts thrust out as they balanced their burden.

Charlotte shook her head in awe. They were so lifelike, so real. She lifted her hand to trace the curl of the hair of the closest maiden where it rested against her rounded cheek, her strong jaw contrasting with a bold nose that—

Charlotte gasped. "That's—I'm—" She stepped back, almost stumbling in her haste. "That's *me!*" She lifted her lamp toward the other figure and gasped again as her face stared back at her from that pillar, as well. Both of the nearly nude figures were of her.

She didn't know whether to laugh or cry or shout or—

A flash of light sparkled outside, near the window. Muttering threats to the absent Marco, she left the fireplace to peer outside, pushing aside the heavy curtains. The strange lights had reappeared and now the entire lawn was filled with them. As she watched, they moved toward the woods, disappearing from sight, one at a time.

First thing in the morning, she'd speak to Marco about the fireplace, but for now, she had a far more pressing errand. Carrying her lamp, she left the dining room and hurried out of the Hall, closing the door quietly behind her. The cool evening air clung to her skin as she walked across the dew-spun lawn and into the darkness of Balesboro.

~

Marco rubbed his neck and looked around the nearly empty work shop. His work was done. The fireplace surround had been installed, and needed only a little plaster to fill in the few cracks where the marble met the wall. Then, the real work would begin when he and Charlotte faced their families and began their life together as—

He frowned. *I didn't ask her to marry me. That is what she wants, isn't it?* God knew, it was what he wanted. He'd assumed she would wish to marry, but Charlotte was full of surprises and he knew not to take anything for granted.

Distracted, he went to shut the door, his mind twirling around plans involving rings and surprises, when a light caught his eye.

He stepped into the blackness of the stable yard where, in the distance, a lantern bobbed across Nimway's dark lawn, carried by a person dressed in a long cloak who moved with a telling limp. *Where are you going at this time of the night, little one?*

Wherever she was going, she wasn't going alone. He picked up the lantern hanging over his work table and set off after her, his gaze glued to the bobbing light. *Please don't go into the woods. Of the places I don't want to be at night, these woods would top the list.*

But as usual, she didn't listen. She took the main pathway into the forest. Marco, muttering under his breath about women who wouldn't listen and crazed owls and the deadly danger of uneven pathways, followed. These woods would be the death of him. What had the groom told him? Ah yes. Evil fairies. *Who doesn't enjoy the company of evil fairies?*

Damn that woman! Well, wherever she was going, she was about to have a companion, whether she wanted one or not. Scowling, he found the path she'd taken and followed, his footsteps swallowed by the blackness of the forest.

~

The tiny lights sprinkled, shimmered, and preened, always just far enough ahead to keep her hurrying, almost running. Panting, she hopped across a fallen branch, holding her skirts higher so they wouldn't drag in the damp grass.

Her half boots thudded in the soft forest floor, crunching on sticks as she went, branches grabbing at her skirts, her lantern swinging wildly. The scent of crushed grass and damp night air wafted through the air as she hurried on. In the back of her mind, she could almost see Caroline doing the same thing – hurrying after the light, following it into the wood . . . Was that what happened?

But Caroline had been on a horse. Perhaps she'd thought she would be safer on a horse? Or maybe the light had moved too swiftly to catch on foot?

The light danced way ahead, seeming to balance on the end of leaves and on the tips of blades of grass before diving in a twinkle to the base of a tree. Charlotte hurried on, following the twisting path until, at a turn near a gnarled oak, the lights disappeared as suddenly as they appeared.

"Oh, no, you don't!" She whisked around the path, and came to a halt so fast, her skirts swung forward as she looked around. She'd never seen this particular glen. It was beautiful, a small round clearing in the middle of gentle, swaying trees. The bright moon sparkled on a small silvered pool filled with swaying cattails. In one corner, almost hidden from view, was a thatched crofter's hut that leaned to one side. Inside the windows, lights sparkled and then disappeared, only to sparkle again. *Oh Balesboro, you do like surprises, don't you?*

She walked toward the hut, her boots crackling on fallen twigs. What could be in the—

"What in the hell are you doing?"

She dropped the lantern, the light extinguishing as it hit the ground. Hand over her thundering heart, she wheeled around.

Marco stood at the edge of the clearing, glowering as if he'd caught her stealing. His dark hair was mussed, his shirt torn at one elbow, a vivid scratch glistened on his forearm.

She frowned. "What are you doing here?"

"I came to keep you from being injured."

She noted where a slow line of blood was soaking into his torn sleeve. "I'm not sure who should be protecting who," she observed.

He didn't so much as smile. "What are you—"

A rustle in the trees made her turn. Marco was instantly at her side, his arm around her waist. She clung to his arm, her cheek pressed against him.

No other noise followed, and finally, she stepped away from him and gave an unsteady laugh. "It's far less friendly here at night."

"Unfriendly? It's dangerous." He growled the words.

"As my sister discovered."

He winced. "I'm sorry. I didn't think." He lifted the lantern and looked around the small clearing. "Is this where the accident happened?"

"I don't know. I never asked. To be honest, I didn't want to know."

"That's understandable. I'm not sure I'd want to know, either."

She sent him a curious look. "How did you know I'd be here?"

"I saw your lantern, and I worried you might come to some

harm. What are you thinking, running into the woods at this time of the night?"

"I saw lights. Dancing lights. Like . . . fairies, or—" She shook her head. "I don't know what they were, but they came this way."

He raised his brows. "Do you see them now?"

"No, but they were in the crofter's cottage when I arrived."

He bent to pick up her lantern. He peered at it and then set it back on the ground. "I was hoping we could relight it, but the cage is bent." He looked past her to the cottage. "Maybe these dancing lights will stay long enough to show you what they want you to see."

She looked at him, surprised. "You believe in fairy lights?"

"You and Nimway have taught me that the impossible can happen."

Her heart warmed, and she slipped her hand in his. "We should look in the cottage and see what's to be found."

His hand tightened over hers and together, they walked to the cottage.

Marco wished the little building wasn't tucked into the corner of the glen, far out of the natural spill of light. He glanced at the trees where they waved overhead, noting that several branches looked at if they might drop at any minute. He sent them a significant glare. *Don't even think about it*, he told them.

He suddenly realized she was watching him, a smile curving her mouth. "What?"

"You're afraid of Balesboro."

"I am not."

She pursed her lips, still looking far too amused.

He scowled in mock outrage. "This wood will not best me. I—"

An owl hooted and he whirled toward the sound, searching the dark branches overhead.

Her chuckle brought him up short. Slowly, he turned back to face her. "I won't do anything to you here, in this dangerous situation. But once we are safely home, you will pay for every laugh and every giggle."

Her lips curved intro a smile, and he admired the way the moonlight sparkled over her long hair. She hadn't taken the time to put it up, and it hung about her face in loose waves, making her appear even younger.

Still smiling, she continued toward the crofter's cottage. Marco followed, holding the lantern high.

As they neared the cottage, he was unhappy to see that it was far more ramshackle than he'd thought. The shutters hung at drunken angles from their hinges, two of them were missing. The front door was cracked as if someone had kicked it in, and gaping holes showed in the thatched roof. "Are you sure you want to go in there?"

"I have to."

"What? Why do you *have* to?"

"I'm the guardian now. And I think those lights may be what drew Caroline into the woods."

"I see." That explained so much.

"But . . ." Charlotte frowned. "I can't see her following lights the way I did. She was like you, and Balesboro made her uncomfortable."

"I thought you said it protected those from Nimway?"

"It does. It never attacked her the way it does you, but she didn't like to be here alone." In the distance, crickets chirped, and toads sang, but it was quiet here in the glen. "I'll never understand what drew her here. She was afraid of the dark. If she decided to venture into the woods at night – which she would never do – she would have asked me to go with her. Our rooms were right beside each other because sometimes she'd have a bad dream and—" Her voice faltered.

"She'd come to you."

Charlotte nodded, the moonlight rippling over her loose hair. "She was the pretty one, but to her, I was the brave one. She believed I could do everything she couldn't."

"Like ride horses."

"Which is yet another thing that makes no sense."

"Do you know what I hear? You have a lot of good reasons to investigate the crofter's hut, but it's dark and late."

Her eyes lifted to his face, almost black in the moonlight.

"You won't find answers in the middle of the night. Come. I'll walk you back to the Hall and we're return tomorrow and face whatever's here together, in the light of day." Marco slid his arm about her shoulders and tugged her closer.

"You think that would be best."

"I do." He turned, but she didn't move.

He stopped and looked down at her. "Charlotte?"

"I'm not the brave one."

The words were whispered, but he heard them as clearly as if she'd yelled them. He was so surprised that he couldn't speak. She was many things – sharp witted (painfully so), independent, frustrating, and unequivocally brave. "Ah, my love, you are indeed brave. You just don't know it." He pulled her closer.

He hadn't planned on kissing her. He'd just thought to ease the emotion he saw darkening her face. But when he pulled her into his arms, she looked up at him.

He could do many things, but resisting her wasn't one of them. Not if he tried a thousand times over. She looked so damn appealing, so sensual, and he bent to place his lips over hers—

Bam! The sole hinge holding the door to the cottage broke and sent the broken wood tumbling.

For a long moment, they stared at it.

Charlotte straightened her shoulders and wiped her hands on her skirt. "I'll be back."

"But—"

She was gone. In two quick hops, she'd leapt over the broken door and disappeared inside the dark cottage.

Cursing, he started after her, but before he could take more than a step, she'd returned. She stood in the doorway, her hands crossed over her chest. At first, he'd thought she might have injured herself, but as she came closer, he realized she was hugging a small book.

When she reached him, she held it out, the moonlight shimmering on gilded letters embossed on leather. With hands that trembled, her eyes shiny with tears, she said, "It's Caroline's diary. Now we'll know why she was in the woods the night she died."

CHAPTER 14

A short time later, Charlotte and Marco slipped into Nimway Hall and silently made their way to the sitting room.

Marco closed the door and placed his lantern on the small table before the fire, watching Charlotte with a concerned gaze. She'd said very little after finding her sister's diary. Her face pale, she perched on the edge of the settee, the book on her knees.

He waited, wondering if she would read it now, but instead she stroked it slowly, her eyes filled with tears.

Marco stirred the fire back to life, and added some wood, careful not to let the poker clang too loudly when he returned it to its hook. When he turned back, Charlotte was hugging the book as if it were a child, rocking slowly back and forth, tears streaming down her face.

He thought of his own sisters and how protective he'd felt of them and how his own heart would break if something happened to them. Never had he felt so helpless.

A sob broke from her and he hurried back to the settee and gathered her to him.

Holding the book to her, she burrowed against him and wept.

She wept until his shirt was soaked with her tears, until she could cry no more, until she'd broken his heart with her own.

Her cries subsided into shuddering sighs and, finally, into soft sniffles. Marco didn't know how to comfort her, so as time passed, he rubbed his cheek against her hair, and whispered to her of his own family, of his sisters and brothers, of the funny stories, and the painful ones. It worked. Her weeping ceased, and she listened, even giving a watery giggle at one point.

It was the sweetest sound he'd ever heard.

Finally, much later, his stories done, he began to yawn. She pulled away and placed her hand on his cheek. "I'm going to read this now."

"Very well. I'll—"

"No. I need to read it alone." She kissed him tenderly. "Please."

"Of course. But I'm not leaving your side."

She nodded.

He piled pillows in one corner of the settee, and sat down, tucking her against him. And then while she read, he slept.

"Good God!"

Marco opened his eyes, aware of three things at once.

First, Charlotte was in his arms, her warm bottom pressed comfortably against him. *What a lovely way to wake up in the morning.*

Second, someone had thrown open all of the curtains and the sitting room was now flooded with light, which made it hard to see the third thing.

Which were the four faces now staring down at him over the back of the settee.

He squinted against the light, trying to figure out who had disturbed his sleep.

One was a distinguished gentleman with graying auburn hair,

and a pair of suspiciously familiar dark blue eyes. The man looked alarmingly ready to kill someone. *Mr. Harrington.*

Beside him was an older, but still attractive woman dressed in the height of fashion, her still-blonde hair elaborately coiffed, jewels glittering at her ears and throat. Her gaze was pinned on Marco with such intensity that he could feel it sticking him in the ribs like a sword. *Mrs. Harrington.*

To the other side of the woman was a young, dark-haired, slender, well-dressed man, whose expression could only be described as 'confused.' *Is this John, the brother?* Somehow, Marco didn't think so, for there was no family resemblance. *Wait. You're the abominable Roberto, aren't you, my friend.*

It took some effort to keep his scowl to himself.

The last face Marco knew. Lady Barton, as plump and bejeweled as ever, wiggled her fingers at him in greeting. Her eyes brimmed with merriment, her cupid's-bow lips curved in a delighted smile. She said in a spritely tone even though she whispered, "Hello there! Fancy meeting you here."

Mr. Harrington glared at her. "Damn it, Verity, this is not the time for levity—"

"Oh hush, Jack." Lady Barton sent him an annoyed look. "And lower your voice. Charlotte's asleep." Lady Barton turned her smile back to Marco. She bent over the back of the settee and whispered, "Mr. di Rossi, would you like some breakfast? Simmons had just informed us that it was ready when one of the footmen discovered you here."

Charlotte stirred in his arms, murmuring in protest at the noise. Her lashes fluttered open as sleep left her. He knew the second she saw the faces above her, for her eyes snapped open and she scrabbled to her feet, swaying at the sudden movement, the book tumbling to the floor at her feet.

"Good morning, child." Lady Barton beamed as if Charlotte had just done the most amazing thing. "Sleep well?"

Mrs. Harrington favored her sister-in-law with a chilly gaze. "Verity, you have failed as a chaperone."

"You think so?" Lady Barton's gaze traveled slowly over Marco. "I was thinking I did rather well."

Charlotte was frantically trying to set herself to rights, tugging on her skirt, smoothing her straying hair, and in general trying to make herself look less 'slept upon the settee.' "Mama! Papa! When did you get in? I—" Her gaze fell on the young man, who had yet to say a thing. "Robert?" Her voice cracked.

Marco decided it was time he joined the fray, so he stood, only to discover that his shirt had bunched up and had rolled high under his arms. He tugged his shirt back into place, aware that Lady Barton's eyes followed his every move, showing her approval with an enthusiastic nod.

For all the approval Lady Barton was showering on him, Charlotte's ex-fiancé was dousing Marco with a scowl. "You, sir, will answer for this!"

Marco was more than willing, but Charlotte sent him a warning look and then stepped in between them. "Robert, I assume you received my letter."

"I did." The young man dragged his gaze from Marco and turned to Charlotte. Instantly, his face softened. "Charlotte, please! You must rethink this. Everything you said was right. I left as soon as we became engaged, and that's my fault, but—"

"Robert, don't. As I said in the letter, we were never meant to be. And you know it, too."

"Don't be so sure," Mrs. Harrington said stiffly. "Charlotte, this is ludicrous. What are you thinking? That man is nothing more than a common sculptor and—"

"No." Charlotte slipped her arm through Marco's. "He is not a common anything. He's an exceptional sculptor, and soon he will be an exceptional husband and, then, an exceptional father."

Husband. Father. Marco had to fight the desire to sweep her off her feet and give her a kiss she wouldn't soon forget. Sadly, given the circumstances, all he could do was cover her hand with his and squeeze her fingers.

Meanwhile, Mrs. Harrington had paled at Charlotte's words, while Robert flushed a deeper red, his hands fisted at his sides.

Lady Barton clapped in delight as she beamed at Charlotte. "You'll have children! How lovely!" She leaned toward her brother. "They will be beautiful. I mean, just look at them."

Oddly enough, Mr. Harrington was no longer looking surprised, nor even upset. Instead, he now watched Marco with a cool, calculating gaze that made him wish he'd worn his court clothing.

Lady Barton beamed at the small group with all of the pleasure of a hostess greeting her guests at a party. "May I suggest that we retire to the breakfast room? I, for one, am famished. Perhaps some food would not be amiss before we have The Discussion?"

"I am not sitting with this man," Robert snapped.

Charlotte frowned. "Robert, please. You don't wish to marry me. Admit it."

"I'm admitting no such thing." Robert glared over her head at Marco. "This fool and I should step outside and finish this once and for all."

Marco shrugged, willing to go in whatever direction this young hothead wished.

"Verity's right," Mr. Harrington said in a calm tone. "We should repair to the breakfast room and finish this discussion in a calm manner. To be honest, I am starving, too."

Marco was starving as well, so he nodded.

"No!" Mrs. Harrington snapped. "Jack, I am not sitting down with this man for breakfast, or dinner, or tea, or anything else. He's *compromised* our daughter!"

"Really?" Mr. Harrington looked at Marco. "Have you compromised her?"

"She's going to marry me. If that's what you mean by 'compromise,' then yes."

Charlotte, who'd sent him a surprised look, blushed, and then slipped her hand back through the crook of his arm. "I would be glad to marry you."

"I'll get you a ring today," he said under his breath, covering her hand with his.

"I've seen enough." Mr. Harrington turned to his wife. "They are getting married, so there's no more for us to say."

Robert made a muffled noise. "No! They cannot!"

Marco thought he detected tears in the young man's voice.

Charlotte must have heard it, too. She released Marco's arm and bent down to scoop up the diary where it rested by her feet.

The color drained from the man's face and he staggered to a nearby chair, where he sat, gasping, his gaze locked on the book.

"What's this?" Mr. Harrington said sharply.

Charlotte kept her gaze on Robert. "It's Caroline's diary."

Mrs. Harrington's hand stole to her throat and she stared at the small book. "Charlotte, are . . . are you certain?"

"I am. I found it last night."

"And you read it?" Mr. Harrington asked sharply.

She nodded and then crossed to where Robert sat, his hands shaking as if he were in a blizzard, tears streaming down his face. She dropped down before him and slid the book onto his lap. "I'm so very, very sorry. I didn't know. She didn't tell anyone, not even me."

"*Robert?*" Mrs. Harrington said, looking as if the world might tilt over. "And *Caroline?*"

Charlotte never looked away from the weeping man. "They've been in love for years. The night she died, she was on her way to meet him. They were going to elope."

Mr. Harrington slipped his arm about his wife just as her knees gave. He helped her to the settee and placed her on it.

Robert stared at the diary, his tears dampening the cover. "Where did you find it?"

"In the crofter's cottage where you used to meet."

"I should have thought to look there." He ran his hand over the book. "I was to fetch her at midnight, but I suppose she . . . I don't know what happened."

"I know," Charlotte said. "She was so excited that she left early. She took the horse and thought to surprise you on the path. It's the last entry she made in her diary. She's loved you for a long, long time. And you, her."

"Since she was fourteen." He picked up the book and hugged it, his face pale. "She was so beautiful and—" He closed his eyes and took a deep breath. When he could breathe again, he lowered the book to his knees. "You all knew her, too, so I don't need to say more. We'd been talking about getting married for so long, but she wanted to wait, and then she wanted a season before—" He gave a bitter laugh. "I was jealous and wrote her some scathing letters, and all for no reason. She was always true to me. I—I just wish I'd been there for her when she needed me."

Charlotte placed her hand over his. "You did what you could. She was trying to prove herself to you, I think."

"I don't understand," Mrs. Harrington said. "We would have welcomed you to our family. Why didn't she just tell us?"

"She thought she was being romantic," Charlotte said. "For once, she was breaking the rules, and she found it very exciting."

"She'd always wanted to elope, and I didn't have the heart to argue." Robert looked at Mrs. Harrington. "May I take the diary with me? As soon as I read it, I'll bring it back."

She hesitated, but after a moment, she nodded. "Of course."

"Thank you." He turned to Charlotte. "I'm sorry. I asked you to marry me because I thought Caroline would want me to take care of you. And I wanted to do that, not just for her sake, but yours. But I couldn't stand being here at Nimway. I see her everywhere. In every room of this house, in every corner, in every memory I have."

Charlotte hugged him, her heart so full that she could barely speak. Robert was her other brother, she realized. And had he married Caroline, he'd have been one in more than mere name. "You're a dear, good friend, Robert. I'm glad Caroline had you in her life while she was here."

He closed his eyes and held her tight.

After a moment, Charlotte gently disentangled herself and stood, aware of Marco's calming presence nearby.

Papa broke the silence. "Well. That was too exciting of a morning for me. Shall we have breakfast now?"

"Not yet." Mama smoothed her gown over her knees, her color almost back to normal. "We've settled everything where Caroline and Robert are concerned, but there is still something that needs discussing." Mama's cool blue gaze locked on Charlotte before she turned to Marco. "Mr. di Rossi, I understand you have installed the fireplace surround."

He nodded, and Charlotte could tell from the tightness of his mouth, that he was preparing for the worst.

Mama continued, "If you will wait, I will pay you the agreed upon amount. More, in fact. But only if you and your assistants will pack your things immediately and—"

"Olivia?" Papa said, his voice oddly soft.

"What?" Mama snapped.

He pointed to a table by the window.

Everyone turned. There, sitting beside a vase of flowers, was the moonstone.

Mama stood, as white as a sheet. "The orb!"

"Orb?" Charlotte frowned. "I thought it was a mace head."

Mama's gaze locked on Charlotte. "You've seen it before?"

"Many times. Marco says it's a mace head, while Simmons seems to think it's a decorative piece, but he can't seem to figure out where to display it."

"Oh dear." Mama turned to Marco. "And you? You've seen it, too?"

"It came to my workshop where it spilled ink and got in the way."

"That solves that," Papa said, looking amused. "Doesn't it, Olivia?"

For a moment, Mama stared at him as if he had three heads. And then, to everyone astonishment, her lips quirked. "You want me to admit I was wrong."

"That would be a nice beginning," he said, his eyes agleam.

Mama flushed, her smile blossoming for real. "It will never happen."

"We'll see about that," Papa murmured, giving Mama such a loving look that Charlotte blushed.

Aunt Verity sighed. "Jack, please stop. She's had a shock. You're being a brute to expect anything from poor Olivia now. Perhaps, after breakfast and some tea, she might—"

"He's right." Mama smoothed her skirts. "Charlotte?"

"Yes?"

"You may marry your sculptor."

Charlotte exchanged a shocked look with Marco. She turned back to Mama and said in a tentative voice, "Really? I can marry him, and you won't disown me?"

Mama looked shocked. "Disown? Charlotte! I would never do that!"

Papa's brows had lowered. "Surely you already knew that."

"I wasn't sure. Things have been so different since Caroline's death and—"

"Oh Charlotte!" Mama crossed to Charlotte and enveloped her in a hug. "I can't believe you thought such a horrible thing for even one moment, although . . ." She pulled back, tears in her eyes. "I suppose I can see why you might have. We haven't dealt as well with Caroline's death and that's my fault. I became very strict with you, because I was afraid something might happen to you, too. I'm sorry."

"It's been difficult for all of us." She smiled at her mother. "Although I'm still curious about this orb."

"Thank God!" Aunt Verity exclaimed. "I want to know about it, too."

Mama smiled at her sister-in-law. "It's a part of Charlotte's heritage. The orb is . . . I don't know how else to say this, but it's magic."

"Really?" Aunt Verity sent an impressed glance toward the moonstone. "What do you do? Rub it?"

"No! The orb is a part of Nimway, and it appears to the guardian when it's needed."

"Caroline was the guardian," Robert said, his mouth tight as if the words pained him.

"She was. Now, apparently, it's Charlotte." Mama's gaze turned back to Charlotte. "I should have realized that after Caroline's death the Hall might look to you, but I was too busy mourning. Where did you find the orb?"

"It was on the old mantel, the one Marco replaced. I'd never seen it before then."

"The orb only appears to a guardian when the time comes for her to meet her true love. Sometimes, if it's necessary, it even helps a bit."

Marco's warm smile found Charlotte and she smiled. "I suppose you could say it helped." She turned back to her mother. "You've never told me about this."

"I should have. I see that now. But I had my reasons. When I met your father, the orb kept leading him to me, over and over. I knew what it wanted of course, but I hated the thought that the orb was making your father fall in love with me. I wanted him to fall in love with me on his own."

Aunt Verity looked impressed. "The orb can do that? Make someone fall in love with you?"

"I don't know what it can and can't do. But it caused me to doubt my feelings and I didn't want that to happen to either Caroline or Charlotte."

Charlotte nodded. "So you didn't tell us."

"No. There are many stories about the orb. I'll share some of them over breakfast."

"Breakfast," Papa said with a note of relief. "Please."

He held out his arm, but instead of taking it, Mama merely patted his cuff, and then turned to Marco. "Mr. di Rossi, if you don't mind escorting me, I believe Charlotte would like to sit with her Papa, especially as she's to be leaving soon. Aunt Verity, if Robert wouldn't mind escorting you?"

"My pleasure," Robert said, as he hurried to slip the diary into his pocket. He arose and took Aunt Verity's ready arm.

Papa came to Charlotte's side and, together, they watched as Marco bowed and then offered his arm to Mama, his manner as grand as any prince.

"Madame," he said gravely, "it would be my pleasure."

She placed her hand along his arm and allowed him to escort her out of the sitting room, Robert and Aunt Verity falling in behind.

Alone in the sitting room, Charlotte slipped her hand into her father's.

"Don't look so worried," he said, smiling down at her. "He will charm her, and she will start thinking of how children you'll have, and all will be well."

"I hope so," Charlotte said fervently. "For I mean to have him, with or without her permission."

Papa chuckled. "Ever a Harrington, aren't you? I'm sure there will be no objections, not now. Perhaps, to seal the deal, after breakfast we'll all visit the dining hall to see your sculptor's work. If it's as impressive as I expect, that will go a long way toward soothing your Mama's acceptance of your chosen one."

Charlotte had to bite her lip to keep from laughing. "Maybe not. I think we should wait on that." She smiled up at her father. "She's had enough excitement for one day, don't you think?"

EPILOGUE

"Do not move."

"I'm not moving!" Charlotte protested.

"You're talking," Marco pointed out, amusement in his dark brown eyes. "That's moving."

"I only spoke because you said something."

"I said 'Your parents are late as usual.' There's no need to respond to that."

It took every scrap of control she could muster not to answer him, and she was reduced to expressing herself by rolling her eyes.

He chuckled and returned to his drawing.

It was a warm summer day and they were in Marco's workshop, a large square room with huge windows thrown open to let in the warm, Italian sunshine. White silk drapes fluttered in the slow breeze, bringing with it the scent of olive trees and red clay. The house was abuzz as the servants readied for their guests.

She smiled, thinking of her parents. It would be good to see them.

"You're smiling. You're not to smile."

"I was thinking of my mother's reaction to the pillars you carved for Nimway."

A wolfish grin warmed his face. "She never told me I couldn't use her daughter as a model."

"She didn't say you could, either."

He shrugged, obviously pleased with himself. "Many people compliment that piece. It will be there for centuries."

Charlotte didn't doubt it. Marco was becoming famous, his work in great demand. She and her family were proud of him.

Mama's only disappointment was that Charlotte had decided to live in Italy with Marco instead remaining near Nimway Hall. But Mama had the mark of the guardian, too, and loved the Hall. It was well taken care of, and Charlotte felt the house knew it.

Outside, near the stables where Diavolo and Angelica held court, children laughed, the sound catching Charlotte's attention. She wished she could lift up just a bit to see if she could spot Isabel playing with her many cousins.

"What is it, *carissima?* A shadow passed over your face."

"I was just thinking of Isabel. I hope she doesn't suffer from the same things I did. So far, her back seems fine, but so was mine when I was her age and I—"

"Charlotte, don't worry. She is fine." His gaze locked with hers. "And if she's not, then we will address it together. To be honest, there are far worse things that could happen to her. Personally, I love your curves. *All* of them."

She had to smile at that, and when he protested, she tried to wipe it from her mouth, and failed.

Complaining, he continued to draw, and she knew from the direction of his glances that he was now sketching her legs. She watched him from under her lashes, this handsome, successful husband of hers, who continued to surprise her each and every day. He was charming, handsome, a loving father, and an ardent lover. He'd taught her much, this one.

She wished she could move, but knew he wasn't yet ready. To

while away the time, she amused herself with all of the ways she was going to seduce him once she was freed from her pose.

"Now you're day dreaming," he announced with a sigh. "Your expression has grown softer."

She sniffed. "I'm trying not to think about how cold it is."

His gaze moved to her exposed breasts. He tsked. "You *are* cold, aren't you? That will never do." He put down his charcoal, and came to where she reclined upon the chaise, a scarf of the thinnest silk draped over her legs.

"Here. Let me warm you." He placed his knee on the edge of the chaise and gently covered her body with his. "Ah. It is as I feared. You suffer from *colpo di fulmine*, the same as I."

"Is that a disease?"

"It is love."

"Ah. Well, then . . ." She slipped her arms around his neck and held him close. As they always did, they fit together perfectly. "I hope we never recover."

"We never will." Smiling, he nuzzled her neck. "Warmer, my love?"

She sighed happily. "Oh yes. Much."

A NOTE FROM THE AUTHOR

Dear Reader,

A very dear member of my family suffers from scoliosis, much like the heroine here, the effervescent Charlotte Harrington. Scoliosis is the curving of the spine and usually happens to children and young adults during periods of rapid growth, but can occur at other times, as well.

It's a difficult condition and while there's no set 'cure' for it, many people with this condition can function perfectly well without assistance. There are several treatments for scoliosis, none of which are easy. Patients suffer years of wearing cumbersome braces or body casts. If the curvature is severe enough, an invasive surgery can be done to meld metal rods along the spine, which leaves the patient in a body cast for up to six months, and sometimes longer. This would be difficult for anyone, but can be especially trying for someone going through their defining teen years.

Scoliosis is not a new condition. Hippocrates mentions it, and even recommends prolonged time in traction as a method for the correction for spinal curvatures. The first supportive bracing was developed in the 1500s by Ambrose Pare'. His patients were placed into padded iron corsets made with holes to reduce the weight. There are many other pioneers in medicine who addressed this condition, most using various forms of bracing, traction, or surgery.

I've witnessed firsthand the struggle a young person faces when they have a condition that sets them apart from others, and I'm delighted to tell you that Marco di Rossi, the hero of this story, is right when he says that we are all different from one another, and it is those differences which make us beautiful. I know this is true for my beloved family member, too. I wouldn't change her for the world.

If you would like to know more about scoliosis, please visit http://www.scoliosis.org/.

All best,
Karen

DISCOVER MORE IN THE NIMWAY HALL SERIES

DISCOVER MORE BY KAREN HAWKINS

One Night in Scotland
Scandal in Scotland
A Most Dangerous Profession
The Taming of a Scottish Princess

The Maclean Curse Series
How to Abduct a Highland Lord
To Scotland, With Love
To Catch a Highlander
Sleepless in Scotland
The Laird Who Loved Me

The Prequel to the Maclean Curse
Much Ado about Marriage

The St. John Talisman Ring Series
An Affair to Remember
Confessions of a Scoundrel
How to Treat a Lady
And the Bride Wore Plaid
Lady in Red

Just Ask Reeves Series
Her Master and Commander
Her Officer and Gentlemen

The Abduction and Seduction Series
The Abduction of Julia
A Belated Bride
The Seduction of Sara

Novellas in Anthologies
The Further Observations of Lady Whistledown
Lady Whistledown Strikes Back

ABOUT THE AUTHOR

Karen Hawkins is a *New York Times* and *USA Today* bestselling author of over 26 fun and lively Regency historical romances and two humorous contemporary romances. Like Sabrina Jeffries, Julia Quinn, Victoria Alexander, and Suzanne Enoch, Karen's books are renown for their sparkling humor, dashing rakes, independent heroines, and often include freshly retold fairy tales (Cinderella, Sleeping Beauty, Snow White, etc), daring rescues, runaway brides, marriages of convenience, Regency balls, and more! With vivid descriptions, strong characters, and captivating plots, Karen takes her readers from London's Regency ballrooms to the purpled moors of Scotland and beyond.

When not stalking hot Australian actors, pretending to do 'research' while looking up pictures of men in kilts from the Scottish highlands, or teasing her husband (aka Hot Cop) about his propensity to idolize chocolate cake over the other food groups, Karen is busy writing her next book while resting her toes on one of her three large rescue dogs.

Made in the USA
San Bernardino, CA
06 April 2018